'I'm so sorry b ~~can't,'~~ **Rowan** ~~gasped as she pulled~~ **herself free from his arms.**

'You're still in love with Colin?' Ewan sighed, leaning back on his heels.

'No. . yes. . .oh, I don't know,' she murmured, her eyes clouding. 'All I do know is that I don't want to be hurt again.'

'Oh, lass, I'd never hurt you,' he said softly, his blue eyes full of compassion.

She gazed up at him, seeing the kind concern in his face, and then looked away quickly, her heart thudding against her ribs. She wanted him—she knew she did—but she was so afraid, so afraid.

Maggie Kingsley lives with her family in a remote cottage in the north of Scotland surrounded by sheep and deer. She is from a family with a strong medical tradition, and has enjoyed a varied career including lecturing and working for a major charity, but writing has always been her first love. When not writing she combines working for an employment agency with her other interest, interior design.

Recent titles by the same author:

A TIME TO CHANGE
A QUESTION OF TRUST

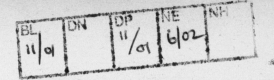

PARTNERS
IN LOVE

BY

MAGGIE KINGSLEY

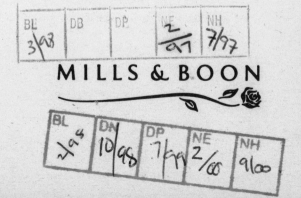
MILLS & BOON

First published in Great Britain 1996
Harlequin Mills & Boon Limited,
Eton House, 18-24 Paradise Road, Richmond, Surrey TW9 1SR

© Maggie Kingsley 1996

ISBN 0 263 15075 5

Set in Times 10 on 11 pt. by
Rowland Phototypesetting Limited
Bury St Edmunds, Suffolk

15-9611-50068-D

Printed and bound in Great Britain
by Mackays of Chatham PLC, Chatham

CHAPTER ONE

ROWAN glanced at her watch and sighed. Half past eight. The other passengers who had got off the train with her at Laith had long since disappeared into the night but still there was no sign of Dr Fowler. Wearily she pushed her fingers deep into the pockets of her sheepskin coat and stamped her feet to try to restore some feeling to them. All in all, it wasn't the most promising of beginnings.

'Dr Sinclair?'

A tall, muscular man of about thirty-five was striding down the frosty platform towards her, a man who was most definitely not Hugh Fowler.

'Yes, I'm Rowan Sinclair,' she said, her eyes taking in a pair of crumpled brown corduroys, a shabby tweed jacket, a harsh lean face and a shock of untidy black hair uncertainly. 'And you are—?'

'Ewan Moncrieff—one of Hugh Fowler's partners.'

Relief flooded through her and she held out her hand with a smile. 'You've no idea how pleased I am to see you, Dr Moncrieff—I was beginning to think I'd come on the wrong day!'

'The name's Ewan and there was an emergency,' he replied, ignoring her outstretched hand and bending to pick up her suitcases.

His voice had a soft Highland lilt to it but there was nothing soft about the decided edge to his words, nor the abrupt way he turned on his heel and set off down the platform, carrying her suitcases. Rowan gazed after his broad back in bewilderment for a second and then hurried after him.

'I'm sorry we didn't have the opportunity to meet

5

when I came to Canna for my interview, Dr Monc—
Ewan,' she declared, catching up with him in the station
car park. 'You were in Fort William at a seminar on
paediatrics, as I recall?'

'Indeed I was,' he replied as he piled her suitcases
into the back of a battered-looking Land Rover. 'In fact,
Hugh made sure I was.'

The irony in his voice was unmistakable and a small
frown appeared on her forehead. Normally she made
friends easily and yet she could almost have sworn that
this man had decided not to like her even before
they'd met.

'The emergency you spoke of—nothing too serious, I
hope?' she continued doggedly.

He closed the back of the Land Rover with unnecessary
force. 'Surprising though it may seem, Dr Sinclair, I
wasn't aware there was such a thing as a trivial emergency, but then I'm only a humble country practitioner,
not a high-flying London doctor like you!'

Rowan's grey eyes flashed and she only just sup-
pressed the angry retort that sprang to her lips. She was
cold, tired, and hungry and perhaps, she thought with
a charitableness she was very far from feeling, Ewan
Moncrieff felt the same. Colin had learned to give her a
wide berth on bad days, waiting until she'd had time to
shower, change and eat before attempting to talk to her.

Her throat tightened as she slipped into the passenger
seat. The past was past. It did no good to remember it.

'Seat belt.'

'Sorry?' she replied, dragging her mind back to the
present.

'Fasten your seat belt,' he ordered. 'This might not be
London but our roads have a plentiful supply of idiots
on them, as I've no doubt you'll soon discover.'

She nodded but her fingers were too cold to function
properly and the seat belt attachment was unfamiliar.

'Let me do that or we'll be here all night,' he said

impatiently, stretching over to clip the metal clasp into its socket.

Instinctively she bent her head to watch the process, only to find that when he straightened up her face was level with his. For a second his eyes held hers and she caught her breath sharply, amazed at the sudden lurch of her heart.

'Thanks,' she muttered in confusion, turning away from him quickly.

What on earth was the matter with her? Nothing about this man should have provoked such a reaction. He wasn't handsome—he was rude and unwelcoming, and he looked as though he bought his clothes at random from the nearest charity shop.

It was his eyes, she realised at last. They were the deepest and most amazing shade of blue she'd ever seen. A wry chuckle broke from her. After that twelve-hour marathon on the train, Kermit the frog would probably have looked good to her right now.

'Something funny?' he demanded, his voice ice-cold.

She bit back her laughter quickly. 'No. . .nothing,' she managed to reply, only to find herself catapulted forward as he released the hand brake with a savage wrench and then drove at breakneck speed out of the car park. 'You were right,' she continued, her laughter bubbling over. 'It didn't take me long to discover there were idiots on these roads.'

'I beg your pardon!' he snapped.

She shook her head, her eyes dancing. 'Save your apologies for that poor cyclist—the one shaking a very irate fist in your direction. I know our patient numbers are small but giving people the fright of their lives seems a rather extreme way of getting new ones, don't you think?'

Ewan's eyes shot to his rear-view mirror and for a split second Rowan thought that he was actually going to laugh, but then his face stiffened. Oh, boy, was he

going to be a fun person to work with, she thought
with a sigh.

Thank God for Hugh Fowler and Matt Cansdale, the
other doctors in the practice. Hugh's enthusiasm at her
interview had been so infectious and as for Matt. . . Her
lips curved. He might be an outrageous flirt but at least
he recognised a joke when he heard it.

As though on cue, Matt's voice suddenly crackled to
life over the car radio.

'Ewan—Charlie Galbraith's had some sort of accident
out at his croft and I'm going to be at Auchbain for at
least another half-hour. Could you take the call, if Rowan
doesn't mind?'

Ewan glanced across at her, his eyebrows raised.

She wanted a bath, a hot meal and her bed but she
knew that she had no choice.

'Take the call,' she said.

He nodded curtly, pulled the car to a screeching halt
and then set off down a bumpy track at a speed that had
her clutching at her seat for support.

It was all so different to what she was used to, she
thought as she gazed out at the passing countryside. She
was used to the excitement of a city that never slept, a
city that was never wholly dark, even in the deepest
recesses of the night.

Here, with the village of Laith left far behind them, the
only sign of human life in the darkness was an occasional
comforting light glinting high on the hills.

Unbidden and unwanted, the warning words of her
boss at the Melville clinic in London came into her mind.

'Are you *insane*, Rowan? You'll be miserable as hell
in a country practice in the Western Highlands, with
nothing but ingrowing toenails, broken arms and measles
to treat. What kind of medicine is that for a girl with
your talents and ability? For God's sake, think again.
Don't throw away your career on the strength of a whim,
and certainly not for the likes of Colin Renton!'

But she'd been adamant that this was what she wanted. She wasn't nearly so certain now, she thought ruefully, and it was all Ewan Moncrieff's fault. If Matt or Hugh had picked her up she was sure she wouldn't be having second thoughts.

'This is it,' Ewan announced as he drew the car to a halt beside a broken-down picket fence. 'Are you coming in or staying in the car?'

Rowan stared out into the darkness and saw a large, ramshackle house, totally surrounded by the rusty remains of ancient vehicles, piles of old tyres, sheets of corrugated iron and abandoned rolls of barbed wire. If this was what the outside of the house looked like, she thought with dazed amazement, what on earth must the interior be like?

'I said, are you coming—?'

'I heard you the first time,' she interrupted. 'And, yes. . .yes, I'm coming with you.'

Quickly she scrambled out of the car, silently cursing her high heels, and followed him up the uneven path leading to the house, only to be half blinded by light as the front door was thrown open by a huge woman in her late forties.

'Come away in, Dr Ewan,' she said loudly, ushering them down a hallway that was a tangle of abandoned wellingtons and broken boxes. 'And you must be the Dr Sinclair we've all been hearing about?' she added, gazing at Rowan with keen interest.

Rowan barely had time to reply that indeed she was before she found herself in a room that seemed, on first impression, to be overflowing with men.

'My sons, Dr Sinclair,' Mrs Galbraith said proudly, seeing her expression. 'Where's your manners, boys? Say hello to the lady doctor.'

Six tall young men, ranging in age from twenty-three to seventeen and all as red-headed as their mother, got to their feet, mumbled a greeting and then sat down again and stared at Rowan with frank curiosity.

'What have you been up to this time, Charlie?' Ewan asked as he strode across to the fire, where a small, whippet-like man was sitting.

'The wife should no' have bothered you,' the man replied apologetically, his face white and pinched and his hand swathed in a makeshift bandage through which blood was clearly seeping. 'I was mending the tractor and the wrench slipped—it's nought but a scratch.'

'I think I should be the best judge of that, Charlie,' Ewan declared, carefully unwrapping the bandage.

The wound was deep and ragged.

'It needs stitches, Charlie.'

'Can you no' just clean it up a bit and put on a fresh bandage, Doctor?' he protested. 'I've that much work to be getting on with I can't be doing with being held back.'

'It needs stitches, Charlie,' Ewan said firmly. 'They'll dissolve in about ten days but you're to do no more work with this hand for at least a fortnight—do you hear me?'

Charlie Galbraith nodded but Rowan could tell from Ewan's deep sigh as he opened his medical bag that he had little faith that his orders would be obeyed.

'You'll take a cup of tea and some of my fruit cake, Dr Sinclair?' Mrs Galbraith asked as she lifted a basket of laundry from the settee to make room for her.

'That would be lovely,' Rowan smiled, thinking how distant a memory the two ham rolls she'd had on the train now seemed, but as Robbie Galbraith—the youngest of the family—was fondly but firmly instructed to get it for her, she could not help but think that she'd never ever been in a house quite like this before.

Curtains hung drunkenly for the want of a few hooks, abandoned cups jostled with tools on the crowded mantelpiece and bits of machinery lay scattered on the floor. A health visitor would have had apoplexy, and as for her boss at the Melville clinic—!

She only just choked down her laughter at the thought

of what he would have said, and yet nowhere on Ewan
Moncrieff's dark, lean face could she see the least sign
of disapproval.

'You're from London, I understand, Doctor,' Mrs
Galbraith observed, settling her ample girth on a stool
by the fire. 'And you worked in a big clinic down there?'

Rowan gazed at her with ill-concealed surprise and
heard Ewan chuckle.

'I should have warned you about the jungle telegraph,
Dr Sinclair,' he said, pausing in the middle of his sutur-
ing. 'By the end of the week I guarantee the entire
neighbourhood will know what brand of underwear
you wear.'

'Oh, that's a terrible wicked slur!' Mrs Galbraith
replied with a deep throaty laugh. 'We'll no' be able to
do that, and well you know it.'

'You mean it will take you all of a fortnight?' he
exclaimed. 'Shame on you, Annie—the telegraph's
surely slipping!'

Rowan glanced across at him quickly. So he did have
a sense of humour, did he? And when he laughed it was
like looking at a different man. His face became gentler,
kinder and, she thought with a disturbing tug at her heart,
unsettlingly attractive. Unconsciously she shook her
head. She had definitely been on that damn train for far
too long!

'Jamie McNeil must be pleased you're renting his flat
over the newsagent's shop in Canna, Dr Sinclair,' Mrs
Galbraith continued. 'It's been vacant since long
enough.'

Rowan paused in the middle of helping herself to a
slice of cake. Ewan was right—the jungle telegraph *was*
good round here.

'I don't know if he's pleased or not, Mrs Galbraith,'
she said. 'I've not actually seen him or the flat yet,' she
explained as the woman's eyebrows rose. 'Dr Fowler
arranged everything for me.'

'Did he now?' Mrs Galbraith replied with an expression that Rowan couldn't fathom. 'So you're keen on the DIY, then?'

Rowan gazed at her in some confusion. 'No—not particularly. Why would I be keen on—?'

'We'd better be heading back to Canna, Dr Sinclair,' Ewan declared, pointedly getting to his feet. 'You must be tired after your journey.'

She was tired and yet, as Rowan made her way to the door with a backward glance of longing at the cake she'd been forced to abandon, she had the strangest feeling that his words owed more to a desire to put an end to Mrs Galbraith's conversation than from any genuine concern for her welfare.

'So, what did you think of the Galbraith family?' he asked as they drove away.

'They need help, that's for sure.'

'Help?' he echoed, puzzled.

'Well, it's pretty obvious everything's getting on top of them,' Rowan observed. 'One look at that house is enough to tell you that.'

'I have a great deal of respect and liking for the family,' he said slowly. 'Everything that can go wrong does go wrong for them. In a thunderstorm their barn is bound to be the one struck by lightning. If there's an outbreak of lung fluke you can rest assured the Galbraiths' sheep will be the worst affected.

'And yet they never complain—they always make light of their disasters.'

'Which makes it all the more obvious they need help, surely?'

'They manage.' His voice was abrupt, clipped.

'I've no doubt they do, but think how much better they'd manage with professional help,' she declared.

The frown line between his dark brows deepened perceptibly. 'We'd better get on to Canna—you must be wanting to get settled in.'

The subject of the Galbraiths was clearly closed as far as he was concerned and she couldn't understand him. If they'd been her patients she would have sent in a social worker and health visitor to help them, not simply admired their stoicism. She sighed deeply. This practice certainly needed the injection of some new ideas, that was for sure.

They didn't reach Canna until a little before a quarter to ten and it was a very weary Rowan who made her way up the stairs beside the newsagent's shop to her flat but, when Ewan flicked on the lights and stood back to let her go in ahead of him, her feelings of fatigue were very quickly replaced by those of horror.

No wonder Mrs Galbraith had asked if she was keen on DIY, she thought as she stared around in disbelief. Jamie McNeil's flat had to be the most utterly depressing place she'd ever seen. Every room was papered with the same dreary brown flock wallpaper, the furniture was huge and ugly and if there was any heating on it was making no impression at all on the chilly air.

Hugh Fowler had said that he'd found her the perfect place, but no one in his right mind would ever have described this flat as perfect.

'Well—what do you think?' Ewan asked, dumping her suitcases down unceremoniously in the middle of the sitting-room.

She turned, fully intending to tell him exactly what she thought, only to bite back the words. He wants me to complain, she thought as she gazed at him. He wants me to say I'm not happy, and something told her that would be the very worst thing she could do.

Deliberately she forced a smile to her lips. 'It's. . .fine.'

That her reply astonished him was clear, but there wasn't just astonishment on his face—there was frustration there, too. What on earth was going on inside this man's head? she wondered in bewilderment. He looked for all the world as though she'd deprived him of a row he'd been eagerly anticipating all day.

'God, what a dump!'

She whirled round, startled, and then a wide smile lit up her face. 'Matt—I hadn't expected to see you tonight!'

'I brought you this to welcome you to Canna,' he replied, indicating the bottle of wine in his hand, 'but I think a bulldozer might have been more acceptable! Ellie. . . Ellie, come and look at this.'

The practice's receptionist, a small plump girl with large brown eyes and shining black hair cut into a bob, appeared in the doorway behind him.

'Strewth!' she exclaimed as she peered round his tall frame. 'Talk about Hammer House of Horrors!'

'It's not easy to get accommodation in our area, Ellie,' Ewan said quickly.

'I know, but—'

'It's fine, honestly,' Rowan interrupted. 'All it needs is a lick of paint and. . .and. . .'

'A bomb?' Matt suggested.

She chuckled. At least Matt Cansdale hadn't changed since she'd met him in the autumn.

'Aren't you supposed to be on call tonight?' Ewan declared, shooting him a terse glance.

'I am and I have my cellphone with me so there's no need to imply I'm playing truant,' Matt replied with a touch of irritation. 'You know, I can't imagine what Hugh was thinking of,' he continued, raking a hand through his brown hair and gazing round with distaste. 'Surely he could have come up with something better than this for Rowan?'

Out of the corner of her eye Rowan saw a faint flush of colour appear on Ewan's cheeks and suddenly knew with absolute certainty and growing anger that Hugh Fowler hadn't found this flat for her—Ewan had.

'Look, why don't you men make yourselves useful and take Rowan's suitcases through to the bedroom?' Ellie observed. 'I brought a casserole and an apple tart with me, knowing Rowan wouldn't feel much like cooking. While they're heating, we can open Matt's bottle of wine. After a couple of glasses this place might start to look halfway decent.'

Matt's eyebrows rose. 'If we're aiming for that I'd better go down to the pub and buy a crate.'

Rowan laughed and saw a frown appear in Ewan Moncrieff's blue eyes.

'I'm afraid I can't stay,' he said. 'I've things to do at home—'

'All of which I'm sure can wait,' Matt exclaimed, bending to pick up one of the suitcases. 'Stay and have dinner with us—it'll give you and Rowan a chance to become better acquainted.'

Ewan's expression suggested that any form of medieval torture would probably have been infinitely preferable, but he managed a small, tight smile before he followed Matt through to the bedroom.

'Friendly, isn't he?' Rowan observed with a sideways grimace at Ellie.

'He's probably tired—you know how it is,' the girl replied, but Rowan had the distinct impression that she knew more than she was saying.

'Ellie—'

'I'll give you twenty minutes to freshen up and then I'll dish—OK?' she declared.

Rowan nodded but she was back in the sitting-room in under fifteen—the coldness of the bathroom saw to that. Matt grinned at her but Ewan merely gave her a curt nod, so deliberately she shot him a beaming smile— a smile, she noticed with gratifying malice, that took him completely aback. Washed and somewhat refreshed, she felt able to tackle anything—even him.

'How was your journey?' Ellie asked as she handed her a plate brimming with meat and vegetables.

'Tiring,' she admitted. 'And it was quite a shock when I got off the train at Laith—I hadn't expected it to be quite so cold, even though it's January.'

'If you think this is cold, Dr Sinclair, you're in for a pretty rude awakening when winter really sets in,' Ewan declared. 'We're in the north of Scotland here, not some mild southern county.'

She gritted her teeth. He was starting again, deliberately putting her down for no reason.

'Since when did we become so formal, Ewan?' Matt demanded, glancing quickly from him to Rowan with a slight frown. 'Her name's Rowan, remember?'

Ewan's lip curled. 'My apologies, Rowan. I keep forgetting we're all just one big happy family.'

Rowan took a steadying breath. Just one more sarcastic comment, she told herself, just one more and I'm going to give him such an earful, first night here or not.

'I thought it was pretty cold today,' Ellie declared with an encouraging smile. 'In fact, I wouldn't be at all surprised if we got snow soon and then we'll have our work cut out.'

'You mean accidents on the road—that sort of thing?' Rowan commented.

'The real problem is the number of inexperienced climbers from down south who take to the hills,' Matt sighed.

'But how does that affect the practice?' she asked, attacking her stew with relish.

'We have an arrangement with the Mountain Rescue,' he explained. 'If there's an accident one of us goes out with them. That won't be a problem for you, will it?'

Ewan was watching her and she swallowed the lump of meat in her mouth with difficulty.

'No. . .no problem,' she said brightly, though her stomach had tightened into a hard knot of panic.

Mountain Rescue—that meant going up hills, high hills, didn't it? And she got giddy on top of stepladders. Why, oh, why hadn't Hugh Fowler told her?

'This casserole's great, Ellie,' Matt observed. 'I don't

suppose there's any chance of a second helping—? Oh, damn and blast,' he groaned as his cellphone rang. 'Wouldn't you just know it?'

'I'll wrap up some apple tart for you to take with you,' Ellie declared, getting to her feet.

'You're an angel,' he beamed, and Rowan saw the girl's cheeks pinken.

So Ellie was keen on Matt, was she? Well, there was a lot to like about him, she decided, but whether he'd ever settle down with just one woman was highly debatable.

'Thanks for the wine and the welcome, Matt,' she said as he made his way to the door with Ellie.

'Hey, anything for a beautiful lady,' he grinned.

She chuckled but as the clock on the mantelpiece struck half past ten the smile on her lips died. Colin would be home now, home to a dinner that he would be sharing with someone else—not her.

Everyone had said they were the perfect couple—he a successful accountant and she a doctor with excellent prospects. They had lived together for two years and she had thought they were happy. It had been Colin who had decided that they were not.

He had grown tired of her arriving home breathless and late when she was supposed to be hosting a dinner party for his clients; tired of tearing theatre tickets to shreds when she'd phoned to say that she'd been asked to change shifts unexpectedly.

Little by little the arguments had begun, and then the recriminations, until one night he'd told her that he would get more satisfaction taking a medical book to bed and then he'd simply walked away.

'More wine?'

She looked up in confusion, forgetting for a moment where she was, and found Ewan's eyes on her, curious, thoughtful. Defiantly she lifted her chin.

'Yes, thanks.'

She wasn't beautiful, Ewan decided, as he filled her

glass—Matt had been indulging in his usual flattery when he'd said that.

Her nose was too short and her mouth was too wide, but the short brown curls that clustered softly round her heart-shaped face were flecked with shimmering gold and she had the most infectious chuckle he'd ever heard. She also looked completely exhausted and he felt a stab of self-loathing for his previous rudeness.

'You've had a long day,' he said awkwardly.

She nodded warily but said nothing.

He had expected someone sophisticated, experienced, but this girl—woman, he supposed, for Hugh Fowler had said she was twenty-eight—didn't look either. Her clothes might betray her London origins, but the large grey eyes that gazed back at him from under a pair of startlingly black eyebrows were not sophisticated.

She looked vulnerable, he thought with surprise— vulnerable and fragile—and a wave of sympathy flooded through him, sympathy that was very quickly followed by anger. Jenny had possessed that same air of appealing fragility and she had been anything but fragile. Unconsciously his face set.

'I hope you've brought some sensible clothes with you,' he said, his eyes taking in her pencil-slim skirt and high heels with clear derision. 'If you try visiting patients in the country dressed like that, you'll end up in hospital yourself on your first day out.'

Her head came up quickly.

'OK, that does it!' she snapped. 'I don't know what your problem is—'

'And I don't know why you've come to Canna, but if you think working here is going to be even remotely like working in an exclusive London clinic you're in for one hell of a shock,' he said coolly.

'I know the situation,' she retorted. 'I know what I'm letting myself in for.'

'Oh, I doubt that—I doubt that very much,' he replied.

'Our surgery should have been demolished years ago, we have a cottage hospital the authorities would like nothing better than to shut and our nearest properly functioning hospital is a two-hour drive away in Fort William. That's the reality of life here, Rowan.'

'I'm not a fool,' she said as calmly as her rising temper would allow. 'I know working here isn't going to be quite the same—'

' "Isn't going to be quite the same"?' he echoed, his blue eyes cynical. 'Lady, this is shoe-string medicine, where the local kids and their mothers hold jumble sales and do sponsored walks if our cottage hospital needs something as basic as a new incubator.

'This is the cutting edge of the National Health Service, where we have to take important decisions damn nearly every day with precious little backup and in the full knowledge that if anything goes wrong we carry the can.'

'And you don't think I can carry the can—that's it, isn't it?' she exclaimed furiously. 'Well, if you're so damned sure I'm useless, why the hell did you appoint me?'

He leant back in his seat, his face hard. 'I didn't. Hugh wanted you and he's the senior partner.'

'And Matt?' she demanded.

'Matt would have been quite happy with a trained chimpanzee if her legs had been good enough.'

Livid colour flooded her cheeks. 'How *dare* you!'

'I dare, Rowan, because the last thing this practice needs is a passenger, a doctor who is going to fall apart when the latest in high-tech equipment isn't available every minute of the day,' he said evenly.

'Hugh made a mistake in appointing you and it's something I'm going to have to live with until you discover you can't cope and go crying back to London on the first available train.'

She gripped the stem of her wine glass until her

knuckles showed white and her voice, when she spoke, was like a whiplash.

'You really are an insufferably smug bastard, aren't you? Without knowing me, without seeing my work, you've judged me and found me wanting. Well, hear this, Mr High and Mighty Ewan Moncrieff—I'm here and I'm going to stay here, whether you like it or not, so you'd better get used to the idea!'

He got to his feet, his expression so thunderous that for a split second she wondered if he was actually going to hit her.

'I presume morning surgery starts at nine?' she said, meeting him glare for glare.

He opened his mouth, muttered what she took to be an assent and then swung out of the room, almost colliding with Ellie on the threshold.

'What's on earth's happened?' Ellie asked, bewildered, as they heard the front door slam shut.

Rowan clenched her hands together tightly to stop them shaking. 'I've just been told in no uncertain terms that I shouldn't have come here.'

'Ewan said that?' Ellie exclaimed, wide-eyed.

'That and a whole lot more I wouldn't care to repeat.'

Ellie shook her head and sighed. 'I knew he wasn't keen to have you join the practice but I thought he'd got over that. Look, he'll come round. I'm sure he will,' she added, seeing Rowan's deep frown. 'Once he realises you came here with the best of motives, he'll accept you.'

Rowan turned quickly to hide the tell-tale flush of colour creeping across her cheeks.

She knew in her heart that she would never have taken this post, in what was effectively a medical backwater, if it hadn't been for Colin. When he had walked out on her all she'd wanted was to get away, to go somewhere where no one knew her, where there were no sympathetic faces. When she'd seen the Canna post advertised she'd jumped at it as though it were a lifeline.

'I think Hugh Fowler and I had better have a long talk tomorrow morning,' she said.

'But he's not here—he's in Canada on a six months' sabbatical,' Ellie declared. 'He thought it a perfect time to go, with you joining the practice. Didn't he tell you?'

Rowan shook her head. There seemed to be a hell of a lot of things that Hugh hadn't told her and, looking back on her interview with him, she wasn't surprised. Nice man though Hugh had appeared, she'd had the distinct impression that he would run a mile rather than face any argument. Her lips curved into a wry smile. In this case, he'd run approximately two thousand miles.

'At least Matt likes you,' Ellie commented, her eyes fixed on her.

'I'm a woman and I'm breathing—of course he likes me,' Rowan observed and saw Ellie laugh. 'You're keen on him, aren't you?'

The girl sighed. 'For all the good it does me. I'm just good old dependable Ellie, as far as he's concerned. And it's probably just as well,' she added with determined briskness. 'Matt likes to play the field and my heart bruises pretty easily.'

'Join the club,' Rowan replied and then bit her lip at having revealed more than she'd intended, but Ellie just nodded sympathetically and began gathering up the dirty plates. 'No, leave those, Ellie,' she said quickly. 'I'll do them tomorrow.'

'You're sure—?'

'Positive. Thanks for the food and the welcome,' she continued as they walked together to the door. 'I appreciate it.'

'Hey, it's no big deal,' Ellie beamed. 'And as for Ewan—give him time. He'll come round.'

'Before I collect my pension?'

A burst of laughter came from the receptionist. 'Well, at least you haven't lost your sense of humour,' she exclaimed.

And, boy, am I going to need it, Rowan thought as she went back to her sitting-room.

Her flat was a dump, her senior partner had decamped to Canada without even telling her that he was going and Ewan Moncrieff would only be happy when he was putting her on a train back down to London.

'Oh, Rowan, what have you done?' she groaned. 'What in God's name have you done?'

CHAPTER TWO

'YOU can get dressed now, Mr Mackenzie.'

Rowan's smile was encouraging, but a pensive frown appeared on her forehead as she went over to her desk. Alec Mackenzie's symptoms seemed to suggest that he was suffering from nothing more serious than a bad bout of flu, but she wasn't happy and she couldn't say why.

Quickly she glanced through his case notes. 'Where do you work, Mr Mackenzie?'

'Frank Shaw's farm over by Dunscaig,' he replied as he came out from behind the screen. 'I used to work for the council, but I got made redundant two years ago. The farm's fine and healthy work, Doctor—out in the fresh air all the time.'

Was it her imagination or did he sound defensive?

'How did you get all those cuts on your hands?' she asked curiously, only to see them disappear under the desk.

'It's part and parcel of the job, Doctor,' he said, his face stiffening slightly. 'No one said farming was easy.'

She nodded. 'You keep your tetanus jabs up to date, I hope?'

'Never miss a one, Doctor.'

She consulted his notes. It was true—he didn't. Perhaps she was overreacting; perhaps he was just suffering from flu, but—

'I'd like to take a blood sample, Mr Mackenzie. It's nothing to worry about,' she added quickly, seeing him go pale. 'Just a routine precaution—'

'Can't you just give me some antibiotics?' he protested. 'That's what Dr Ewan gave Fergus Innes, and he had the same symptoms as me.'

23

'Perhaps he did,' she said evenly, 'but I'd still like to take a blood sample.'

Alec Mackenzie got to his feet. 'I think I'll come back tomorrow—when Dr Ewan's on duty. No offence meant to you, Doctor.'

'None taken, Mr Mackenzie,' she said, though she could feel her cheeks burning, 'but I really would recommend you have that blood test—and I'm sure Dr Ewan would, too.'

He stared at her indecisively for a moment and then backed towards the door. 'I don't have time today.'

'Mr Mackenzie—'

It was too late—he had already gone—and she threw down her pen angrily.

This was the third time this had happened—a patient making it plain that they'd rather be treated by Ewan than by her. It was inevitable, of course. Patients didn't like change, they preferred continuity, but on this occasion she had the distinct feeling that it was more than that.

She'd ask Matt about Alec Mackenzie. She'd ask Matt but she sure as heck wouldn't ask Ewan. She wouldn't ask Ewan the time of day at the moment.

Slowly she made her way out of her consulting-room, only to walk straight into Ewan who was deep in angry conversation with Ellie.

'What do you mean, Bob King hasn't turned up?' he demanded. 'He was due for his check-up today.'

'He didn't keep his appointment, Ewan.'

'Then ring him. Tell him I want him here tomorrow— no excuses. It's essential after his heart operation that we monitor his weight, blood pressure and heart rate.'

'I'll try,' Ellie declared, 'but you know what Bob's like. He hates leaving his shop.'

'Tell him if his backside isn't on my consulting-room chair tomorrow morning I'll come down to the shop— he'll know what that means.'

'A bawling-out in front of his customers!' she giggled.

He shot her a smile, the vivid smile that was so attractive—the smile that's never directed at me, Rowan thought with irritation.

'Practice meeting in the staff-room in ten minutes, Rowan,' he said, noticing her.

'I won't forget,' she replied sweetly as Ellie bustled off to the office.

How could she forget? They had the damn meetings every morning. They were important, of course, she knew that. With the practice covering such a large area, they might all have gone for days without seeing one another but, frankly, if she never saw Ewan Moncrieff she would have been quite happy.

'Ellie tells me you haven't filled in your requisition forms yet,' he continued.

'And Ellie has no doubt also told you I'm doing them this afternoon,' she declared.

His eyes narrowed but he said nothing. Round one to me this morning, she thought, striding past him into the staff-room and switching on the kettle with a snap.

The last two weeks had been a nightmare.

Occasionally—just occasionally—Ewan had allowed her to see that he could be a likable human being but those moments had been rare and always she'd had to pay for them later in the form of veiled sarcasm and barbed asides, and she was getting tired of it—heartily sick and tired of it.

'A penny for them?' Ellie exclaimed as she came into the staff-room and raided the biscuit tin.

'The air would be blue if I told you what I was really thinking,' Rowan replied, taking some cups down from the cupboard.

Ellie sighed. 'It's not getting any better, then— between you and Ewan?'

'No,' Rowan replied tightly, spooning some coffee into the cups.

'He's a good doctor, Rowan.'

He was. Never had she seen the least flicker of impatience or irritation appear on his face when he was dealing with patients, no matter how long it took for them to tell him what was really wrong.

At the Melville time had been of no importance because each patient had been paying—and paying handsomely—for the consultation, but Ewan didn't have that motivation. He was just genuinely interested in people, treating each as an individual—a person who was entitled to his complete and utter attention. Unless that person's me, Rowan thought with a wry inner sigh.

Ellie shut the staff-room door quickly and sat down.

'Ewan's never been an easy man to get to know,' she commented. 'He's had the odd girlfriend, of course—'

'Odd being the operative word, if they went out with him,' Rowan replied with feeling.

'Oh, come on, Rowan, he's pretty darned attractive!' Ellie laughed. 'If he whistled in my direction I'd find it hard to say no!'

'Well, I certainly wouldn't,' Rowan replied firmly, deliberately crushing down the memory of how her heart had flipped over when he'd smiled at her.

'The only woman he's ever got really close to was Jenny Hannay,' Ellie continued. 'She joined the practice straight out of med school four years ago and she and Ewan became quite an item. In fact, everyone thought they'd get married.'

'So what happened?' Rowan asked, well aware that she shouldn't be encouraging the receptionist to gossip, but interested, nevertheless, in discovering anything that might explain Ewan's complex personality.

'No one really knows for sure—which, in this hotbed of gossip, is little short of a miracle,' Ellie frowned. 'All anyone knows is that Jenny only stayed a year and then she took a post down south. As she was really popular the general feeling was that her leaving must have been Ewan's fault.'

'Are you sure it wasn't? I mean, knowing him as well as I do—'

'Knowing who as well as you do?'

Hot colour crept up Rowan's neck at the sound of Ewan's voice behind her.

'Nothing. . .no one,' she said uncomfortably, wondering just how much he could have heard. 'Ellie and I were just discussing a mutual friend, that's all.'

His eyebrows snapped down. 'Where's Matt?'

'I've no idea,' she exclaimed. 'I'm not his keeper.'

'Not whose keeper?' Matt asked as he joined them.

'Yours,' Rowan observed, 'and from what I've heard you sorely need one!'

'Volunteering, are you?' he grinned and Rowan chuckled deeply, only to see Ewan's face set into even more rigid lines.

Oh, get a life, why don't you? she thought with irritation as she took a seat. If he wanted to play the archetypal dour Scot it was his privilege but why, oh, why did he have to inflict it on her all the time?

The meeting wasn't a long one. Various patients were discussed, treatments suggested and then Ewan leant back in his seat.

'Now, if there's nothing else either of you want to discuss, Ellie's asked me—'

'There's something I'd like to discuss,' Rowan declared and saw him put down his papers with ill-concealed impatience.

Well, he could look as discouraging as he wanted to, she decided. She was going to say what was on her mind, come hell or high water.

'I'd very much like to start a clinic aimed specifically at the women in the area,' she continued determinedly. 'A sort of Well Woman clinic, doing cervical smears and that kind of thing.'

'Nice idea but it wouldn't work,' Ewan replied. 'Now, as I was saying, Ellie's asked me to say she's finding it difficult to keep the paperwork up to date because some of us are waiting too long to fill in our requisition forms—'

'Just a minute,' Rowan interrupted, her voice tight, 'can't we at least discuss my idea?'

'There's not much point,' Ewan said smoothly. 'As I said, it's unlikely to succeed. Now, these requisition forms—'

'Oh stuff your damn requisition forms!' she flared, her temper breaking. 'What you mean is the clinic won't work because it's my idea!'

'No, that is not what I meant,' he replied and, to her surprise, he didn't look angry but suddenly overwhelmingly weary.

'Look, Rowan,' he continued as she opened her mouth to protest, 'I've lost count of the number of times a woman patient has said to me, "But I thought the pain would just go away, Doctor," or "I couldn't come before because who was going to look after my bairns and my man?"'

His face was dark, bitter. 'If we can't get them to come when there's a real problem, what chance do you think you'll have of getting them to come for routine check-ups?'

'Won't you at least let me try?' she demanded. 'Maybe the women might be more willing to come to a female doctor than to you or Matt?'

'She's got a point, Ewan,' Matt observed.

'Let me try, Ewan—please—just for a couple of months,' she declared. 'It's my own time I'm giving up and if it doesn't work I'll concede defeat.'

He thrust a hand through his black hair, making it even more dishevelled than usual, and sighed.

'OK, you can try and, believe me, I hope to God it works. We've far too many cases of cervical cancer in our area and it's all because the women won't come forward to be tested. They just don't seem to realise that a few minutes' discomfort and embarrassment are a small price to pay for their lives.'

The meeting was over and, as Matt went off to grab a few hours' sleep before evening surgery, Rowan gathered her case notes together quickly, all too aware that Ewan's eyes were fixed on her.

'I really do hope your clinic is a success,' he said unexpectedly. 'It's an idea I had myself some time ago.'

'Great minds think alike, then?' she said lightly.

A rueful smile spread across his face. 'I'm afraid there's another saying and it's not a very encouraging one.'

'Fools seldom differ, you mean?' she chuckled.

His smile deepened. 'It's very generous of you to give up your free time to try it.'

'I don't mind,' she replied as she edged her way to the door, knowing how quickly his mood could change.

'How are you finding the work?'

She stopped in her tracks. 'Fine,' she said warily.

'No problems?'

For a moment she considered telling him about Alec Mackenzie and then rejected it. 'No. . .no problems.'

'You must be finding Canna a bit of a culture shock after the Melville clinic, surely?' he pressed.

'No, not at all,' she insisted.

It was a downright lie. Working in Canna had proved to be a huge culture shock, and the biggest shock of all had been discovering just how much she'd taken the medical facilities at the Melville for granted.

At the Melville she had been able to arrange for a patient to have blood tests, X-rays or even a CT scan, all within a day in the clinic's various departments. Here the slowness of the referral system and the amount of paperwork involved just to get a patient an appointment in Fort William drove her crazy.

'So you've no problems, then?' he continued.

She was tempted to say, only one—you, but didn't. 'No. . .no problems.'

He nodded and she turned on her heel quickly.

'Rowan.'

Here it comes, she thought as she turned back slowly towards him, her mouth tightening. Here comes the gibe—the barbed criticism.

'I know it's a bit of a pain but if you could get those requisition forms done today it would be a great help,' he said.

Was that it? she thought in amazement as he picked up the dirty cups and took them over to the sink. Was that all he was going to say? No sarcastic remark, no put-down? She couldn't believe it and as she made her way back to her consulting-room she decided that if she lived to be a hundred she'd never understand what made this man tick.

It was almost five o'clock before she had finally ploughed her way through the requisition forms, and she was just getting thankfully to her feet when Matt arrived back at the surgery.

'Oh, great, you're still here,' he declared. 'Those reports Ewan's been waiting for from the Fort William lab have just come in. Could you drop them off at his cottage on your way home and get his opinion on them? He should be back from his rounds by now.'

'But I'm on call tonight, Matt.'

'And I've got evening surgery in half an hour. Look, it will only take you ten minutes—twenty, tops—it's no big deal, surely?'

Not for you, it's not, she thought, but Ewan had been nice to her earlier and she knew from past experience what to expect now.

'Can't you do it, Matt?' she asked in her best wheedling tone.

He shook his head with irritation. 'Look, can't you at least try to get on with Ewan?' he demanded. 'I know he's got a sharp tongue and a quick temper, but I tell you this—if ever I was in a jam, he'd be the man I'd go to.'

'Everyone's entitled to one mistake, I suppose,' she replied evenly.

Real anger appeared on Matt's face.

'Ever thought you're not entirely blameless yourself, Rowan?' he exclaimed, throwing the reports down on her desk. 'Think about it when you're delivering these— think about it hard.'

She bit her lip as he strode away from her. Maybe there had been times over the last two weeks when she'd overreacted; maybe she was letting the situation with Ewan get out of hand. Perhaps if they talked and got a few things sorted out, away from the claustrophobic atmosphere of the surgery? It was worth a try.

All of her good intentions faded, however, when she drew up outside Ewan's cottage to find the door firmly locked and no sign of his car anywhere. He could be hours yet and she wanted to go home, to get something to eat, not hang about here.

'Dr Ewan shouldn't be too long, Dr Sinclair,' a voice called out. 'I saw him going into Mrs Fielding's and I think she was his last home visit for today.'

Rowan turned to see Ewan's neighbour, hanging over the fence.

'He keeps his key under that flowerpot,' the neighbour continued helpfully, 'and I'm sure he wouldn't mind if you let yourself in. I mean, it's not as though you'd rob the place, is it?'

For a moment Rowan stood indecisively in the driveway. It was a bitterly cold evening and the thought of waiting outside for him in the car was not an appealing one. Would he mind if she let herself in? The neighbour had said that he wouldn't, nor did she think she'd suddenly be beset with an overwhelming urge to rob him.

Deliberately she retrieved the key and let herself in, only to decide with a rueful chuckle that if she had been a burglar she would undoubtedly have turned tail and fled immediately.

Ewan's sitting-room was a disaster area. Books and clothes were scattered everywhere, dirty plates were clearly visible under several seats and a seemingly endless collection of mugs sat abandoned on the mantelpiece.

The kitchen was even worse. Pots and pans were piled high in the sink, the table was littered with discarded biscuit wrappers and half-eaten cans of beans and sitting on one of the seats was a casserole containing something that the health authority would undoubtedly have condemned on sight.

She supposed that she shouldn't have been surprised. A man who took so little interest in his clothes was scarcely likely to concern himself about his home, and yet she could not help but shake her head wryly.

'Oh Ewan, Ewan,' she murmured, and instinctively reached for the washing-up liquid.

A muttered oath came from Ewan's lips as he recognised Rowan's car in his driveway. All afternoon he'd been looking forward to a quiet, relaxing evening and it was clearly not to be.

Wearily he got out of his car, knowing that there had to have been some emergency to bring her to his door, but when he went into his cottage and found the sitting-room empty a deep frown appeared on his forehead. Where the hell was she, he wondered, and what had happened to the dishes that usually littered the place?

Puzzled, he pushed open the kitchen door and found the answer to both questions. A huge pile of clean dishes and pots sat on the draining-board and Rowan stood beside them—her sleeves rolled up, her hair curling in damp tendrils round the nape of her neck—humming quietly to herself.

A smile curved his lips. It had been a long time since his kitchen had looked like a home, instead of just somewhere to grab a bite to eat. Not since Jenny, he remembered, and at that thought the smile on his lips died. For the last three years he had organised his life into a quiet, predictable routine, and it was a routine he wanted no one to disrupt—no one.

He took a step forward and she must have heard him, for she whirled round quickly and then laughed.

'Ewan—you almost gave me a heart attack!'

'What are you doing here?' His face was cold, shuttered.

'Your neighbour told me where you kept the key—'

'I didn't ask how you got in—I asked what you were doing here.'

'Right at this minute I'm drying these dishes,' she said, beginning to feel slightly uncomfortable. 'I have to say your kitchen's a fine advertisement for a doctor,' she added with a chuckle. 'I'm surprised you haven't gone down with salmonella or dysentery—'

'How I choose to live is none of your damned business,' he interrupted, roughly pulling the dish towel from her grasp. 'No one asked you to come in.'

She gazed at him uncertainly. 'Look, I'm sorry if you think I've intruded—'

'And no one asked you to clean up for me, either,' he continued tightly. 'I do not need a cleaner—or a surrogate mother. And I'm not in the market for a relationship either, if that's what you're thinking.'

She gasped out loud in outrage, hot colour flooding over her cheeks. 'Why, you arrogant, conceited—! Let me tell you this, Ewan Moncrieff. Whatever charms you may have—and quite frankly right at this minute I can't think of a single one—are totally wasted on me!'

He took another step forward, his face a mixture of conflicting emotions. 'Rowan, I think—'

'No—no, you don't!' she interrupted, her grey eyes

hard. 'You just open your mouth and say the first hurtful or insulting thing that comes into your head!'

'Rowan—'

'The only reason—the *only* reason—I'm here is because Matt asked me to drop off your reports and get your opinion on them. I thought rather than sit around waiting for you to come back I might make myself useful. I thought—I *thought*—you might be just a little grateful. Clearly I was mistaken, but I sure as hell won't make that mistake again!'

She didn't give him time to reply. She just reached for her coat and stormed out to her car.

Never had she been so angry, she thought as she rammed her car keys furiously into the ignition. Boiling in oil was too good for him; roasting him over a slow spit wouldn't have given her sufficient satisfaction. Perhaps she shouldn't have cleaned up his precious domain; perhaps he liked living like a pig, but that didn't give him the right to suggest that she—!

'Oh, start, damn you,' she cried as her car spluttered momentarily into life and then died. Desperately she tried again and sighed with relief as the engine started, only to become aware of an insistent tapping at her window. She turned in her seat to see Ewan mouthing something at her through the glass and for a second considered driving away—preferably over his foot—and then changed her mind.

'Thought of some other insult, have you?' she said tartly as she rolled down the window. 'Come up with some other gem you want to share with me?'

'I think. . .I think I owe you an apology.'

'And I think that's got to be the understatement of the year!' she retorted.

He reddened. 'Look, I'm not. . .' He paused, clearly searching for the right words. 'I'm not very good at apologising.'

'You surprise me,' she replied, ice-cold. 'Considering

your obvious lack of manners, I would have thought you'd have had plenty of practice!'

He bit his lip. 'Look, please come back inside. Stay for dinner—we can talk.'

'Are you sure you'll be safe?' she exclaimed. 'I mean, aren't you afraid I'll become so overwhelmed by your irresistible charms that I'll leap on you, rip off all your clothes and force you to make mad, passionate love to me?'

His lips twitched. 'In that case I definitely think you should come back in—it sounds like I could be in for a fun evening.'

She stared at him for a moment and then, despite herself, a reluctant smile was drawn from her. 'You're impossible—you know that, don't you?'

'I know, and I truly am sorry,' he declared. 'Please come back inside.'

'Give me one good reason why I should,' she demanded.

'I'll give you three. Number one, I think we should get a few things sorted out; number two, I'm getting a stiff neck talking to you like this; and number three, we have a very interested audience.'

Rowan glanced round to see Mrs Ross, the fount of all Canna's gossip and the spreader of most of it, watching them curiously from the bottom of the drive.

'All right, I'll come back in,' she said slowly, 'but on one condition only.'

'Name it.'

'We make a deal.'

'A deal?' he echoed.

'I know you didn't want me here—God knows you've made that plain enough over the last two weeks—but if you promise that from now on you'll judge me solely by my work and not by any preconceived ideas you might have about me, then I promise. . .I promise faithfully I won't try to seduce you.'

Real laughter lit up his face. 'I'll agree to the first part but I most certainly won't hold you to the second—I might be an idiot, but I'm not a fool!'

The combination of those eyes and that smile was devastating, she thought as she got out of the car, but she hadn't come north looking for a relationship. She'd come north, hoping that in a new job with new people she might find it easier to forget, and getting involved with a man like Ewan Moncrieff was most definitely not part of the agenda.

'Take a look in the fridge and see if you can find anything that takes your fancy for our dinner,' he declared as he hung her coat up behind the sitting-room door.

She nodded but all she could find in the fridge was some eggs, a pint of milk, four slices of bread and a very sad-looking piece of cheese. She turned to the cupboards. Their contents were more promising, but only just.

'Find anything?' he asked, appearing at the kitchen door.

'We can have eggs on toast, spaghetti on toast or beans on toast,' she observed. 'If we eat anything else I've a feeling we could end up in hospital.'

Acute embarrassment appeared on his face. 'I could go down to the fish and chip shop—?'

She shook her head. 'We won't starve. So, which do you want—the eggs, the spaghetti or the beans?'

'You mean you're cooking?' he exclaimed.

'If this is an example of your culinary skill,' she declared, holding up a pan she had been soaking, 'I think it might be wise, don't you? Unless my offering to cook makes you feel threatened?'

He grinned. 'I asked for that, didn't I?'

'You did,' she smiled. 'So, what's it to be?'

'Poached eggs on toast would be great. Look, can't I do anything to help?' he added as he hovered uncertainly at the kitchen door. 'It seems a bit much to invite you to dinner and you end up cooking it.'

'I wouldn't be cooking if I didn't want to,' she laughed. 'I'm not that noble. Look, these eggs won't take long so why don't you take a look through the reports Matt sent you?'

He nodded and she retrieved the eggs from the fridge with a smile.

It didn't take long to poach the eggs and they ate their meal in companionable silence. To Rowan's relief, Ewan seemed to realise that she did not want or expect conversation. All she wanted was to relax.

'I think I've got some cheese and biscuits to go with your coffee, if you'd like,' he said as he began clearing away their dirty dishes.

'Just a biscuit, please,' she said. 'I've seen the cheese.'

'A bit high, is it?'

'High? I reckon with just a little encouragement it could probably tap-dance its way out of the fridge!'

His face lit up with laughter and she glanced away quickly. This man had put her through hell over the last two weeks—he'd insulted her, for God's sake—and yet she knew that she was beginning to like him, to like him a lot. Deliberately she crushed down the thought. She wanted no complications in her life, no entanglements of any kind.

'I'll make the coffee,' he declared. 'You go through to the sitting-room—put on a record, if you want. There's some by the stereo.'

She went through to the sitting-room with relief and flicked through his records. He certainly had wide-ranging tastes. Some classical, some folk, a few old rock and roll records and some jazz. Extracting a Dinah Washington record, she put it on and then sat down, noticing with a small smile that the sitting-room had suddenly become distinctly tidier.

'So, do you think you'll like working here in Canna, or is it too early for you to pass an opinion?' he asked as he came into the sitting-room, carrying two cups of coffee and a plate of biscuits.

'I'll be a lot happier once my novelty value wears off,' she replied. 'At the moment I can't sneeze without the entire community knowing about it!'

'I'm afraid the interest in you won't ever go away completely.'

She gazed at him in horror. 'You are joking, I hope?'

He shook his head. 'This is a small community and people will always show a lively interest in you and what you do.'

'You mean the famed Highland friendliness is nothing more than good, old-fashioned nosiness?'

'It can seem that way at times, but remember it's that interest in your neighbours that's saved many an elderly person who could have lain ill for days if a "nosy" neighbour hadn't remarked on the fact they hadn't seen them that morning.'

Rowan sighed.

'You don't look too impressed,' he observed.

'It's not that,' she replied. 'It's just I'm not accustomed to such interest and I'm not sure I want to get used to it.'

'You'll have to if you're planning on staying,' he said, gazing at her intently over the rim of his cup.

'Have you always lived here?' she asked, deliberately changing the subject.

'I had to go away to do my training, but I always knew I'd come back.'

'You have family here, then?' she said.

His eyes darkened slightly. 'No, no family. My father was a fisherman—he drowned when I was seven. My mother died of meningitis when I was thirteen.'

'I'm sorry,' she said awkwardly.

'It was my mother's death that made me choose medicine as a career,' he said with an effort. 'I decided then that if I could help it no one else would die needlessly in this area for want of proper care.'

'But you must surely have yearned sometimes to see different horizons?' she asked curiously.

'Absolutely nothing—and no one—would ever make me leave here, Rowan,' he declared, his face suddenly harsh.

'I see,' she replied slowly but, in truth, she didn't see—she didn't see at all.

Beautiful though the area round Canna was, she couldn't imagine spending the rest of her life here; couldn't imagine anyone deliberately choosing to spend the rest of their life here.

'Such dedication must play havoc with your social life,' she observed.

'Medicine plays havoc with your social life,' he smiled. 'It requires a very special person to put up with the broken dates, the disrupted dinners. If they're not secure in themselves they can start to think you're doing it deliberately.'

Don't I just know it, Rowan thought with feeling, but she said nothing.

'I guess I'm quite difficult to live with, too,' he continued.

Downright impossible would be closer to the mark, Rowan thought, but she didn't say that either.

'So, how do you cope—with the pressures of your work and a social life?' she asked instead.

'I've found the best way is to give as little of yourself as possible—that way it minimises the amount of hurt you suffer when it all goes wrong.'

It sounded a very lonely way to live to her, but before she could comment a deep frown appeared on his face.

'I don't know why I'm telling you all this. I don't usually speak about myself.'

'I'm a good listener, I guess,' she smiled.

He shook his head, his blue eyes suddenly cold. 'I'd say you were one dangerous lady, Rowan Sinclair.'

'Me?' she exclaimed, puzzled. 'Why?'

'Because you've managed to find out more about me in the space of an hour than most people do in a lifetime.'

'Perhaps I'd better go, then, before you tell me something you'll regret,' she laughed.

'I think you better had,' he said abruptly, reaching for her coat.

'Hey, I was only joking,' she protested as he all but bundled her to the door. 'What about the reports Matt wanted your comments on?'

'I made notes on them while you were in the kitchen,' he answered, thrusting them into her hand.

'But, Ewan—'

'Thanks for dinner and the cleaning up. It. . .it was kind of you.'

'You're welcome—'

If she'd wanted to say anything else she couldn't have. She was suddenly staring at a firmly closed front door.

Well, that's the first time you've ever been thrown out of someone's house, she thought, half amused, half angry, as she turned and began to make her way down to her car.

He had to be the strangest man she'd ever met. All prickly like a cactus on the outside and yet underneath— She pulled herself up short. She had absolutely no interest in finding out what he was like underneath, she told herself firmly.

CHAPTER THREE

A PUZZLED frown appeared on Rowan's forehead as she recognised Ewan's car drawing in ahead of her at the turn-off to the Wilsons' croft.

'Have we got our wires crossed or something?' she said as he got out of his car and walked back towards her. 'I thought I was doing the rounds and this was your morning off?'

'Right on both counts,' he replied, 'but the Wilsons are friends, as well as patients, and I often drop in to see them. I can come back later, if it bothers you,' he added, gazing at at her.

She shook her head. 'It doesn't bother me,' she said, but it did.

For the last week he had kept his promise to judge her solely on her work, but it hadn't led to an easier working environment. Indeed, if anything, she felt even more uncomfortable in his presence. Whenever she looked up at staff meetings his eyes seemed always to be on her; when she turned round he seemed always to be there. It was, she thought ruefully, rather like sitting on a time bomb and waiting for it to explode.

'Why don't we walk up to the Wilsons'?' he suggested. 'It's not far and I could do with the exercise.'

'Snap,' she answered. 'Every patient I visit practically force-feeds me with tea and cakes, and if I carry on eating like this I'll end up like a balloon!'

'You could do with the addition of a few more pounds,' he commented, his eyes travelling over her. 'You're much too thin, as it is.'

To her acute annoyance, she felt herself blushing.

'Nevertheless, I'm going to have to start refusing some

41

of these offers of tea and cakes,' she said firmly, slipping out of her shoes and into a pair of wellingtons, for the road ahead was frosty. 'I can't stand the pace.'

'Don't do that,' he said, his face full of genuine concern. 'You'd be amazed at what you can learn over a cup of tea. It could be a worry the patient hasn't had the courage to voice, or the discovery that someone else in the family is giving cause for concern.'

'But do I have to eat all the time just to get to the facts?' she protested. 'If I do *I'll* be the one requiring medical treatment!'

He smiled. 'OK, I give you permission to politely refuse the cakes, but always accept a cup of tea or coffee and stay for a while.'

It was a beautiful day for a walk, the sky blue and clear, the ground crunchy underfoot from last night's frost. When she'd come for her interview in the autumn Hugh had given her a guided tour of the area, and the trees had been a spectacular riot of gold and red, the hills stunningly covered with purple heather.

Now the trees were gaunt black shapes against the sky and the heather was brown and dead. It was an alien landscape, stark and darkly brooding, but strangely there were days when she felt almost as though she belonged here, had always belonged here.

'What a stunning view,' she murmured, shielding her eyes against the low winter sun to gaze at the sparkling sheet of water that was Loch Shiel and the high hills beyond.

'Today it is, and that's the mistake many people make when they decide to move here,' Ewan replied. 'They forget about Highland winters. A couple of bad ones are usually enough to send them scurrying back down south.'

Her jaw set and he shook his head. 'Don't get paranoid on me, Rowan. When I said ''many people'' I didn't mean you.'

'Can you blame me for thinking you did?' she

demanded. 'You've done nothing but remind me that I'm an outsider here ever since I arrived.'

'We struck a deal, remember?' he replied. 'I've every intention of keeping to my side of the bargain, and as for your promise—'

She glanced up at him quickly and her heart gave a treacherous leap.

'What about my promise?' she said.

His dark face broke into a grin. 'I live in hope you'll break it.'

'I wouldn't suggest you hold your breath,' she replied lightly, and quickened her pace as he laughed.

It was quite ridiculous the effect this man had on her, she thought crossly as she picked her way up the road that was little more than a rough track, strewn with boulders. One minute she could cheerfully have throttled him and the next— She shook her head. She was just fragile and susceptible after Colin—that was all there was to it.

'Tell me about Geordie Wilson,' she said deliberately.

'He's eighty-five and his wife, Tilly, is eighty-two. They've lived here all their married life, crofting the land with no outside help at all.'

'And Mr Wilson has lung cancer?'

'He has.'

His reply was abrupt and Rowan would probably have questioned him about it if her eyes had not been captured by the Wilsons' cottage.

It looked like something out of a Scottish Tourist Board advertisement, she thought with delight. Small, whitewashed and in a stunning setting—it was Grannie's Heilan Hame come to life. In fact, there was only one thing to mar it, as far as she was concerned, and that was the presence of a very large and decidedly unfriendly looking goat, tethered in the garden.

'Nervous?' Ewan said softly, his blue eyes dancing as

she gave the animal a very wide berth on her way up to the front door.

'Just careful,' she said, and was rewarded by one of the brief, swift smiles that so lit up his face.

'I didn't expect to see you today, Ewan,' a tiny, elderly woman exclaimed as she came out of the cottage, a welcoming smile on her face. 'And who's this bonny stranger with you?' she continued, gazing at Rowan, her eyes sparkling with interest.

'The newest member of our practice, Tilly—Dr Rowan Sinclair,' he replied.

Mrs Wilson's face fell. 'And there was me thinking you'd found yourself a nice young lady at last,' she sighed. 'Aren't you ever going to settle down and get married, lad?'

'Now, how can I do that when the one woman I've ever wanted to marry is married already, Tilly?' he replied sadly.

Rowan glanced across at him in surprise and so, too, did Mrs Wilson.

'Well, all I can say is she must have been a fool if she turned you down,' Mrs Wilson declared stoutly.

His eyebrows rose. 'I wouldn't call you a fool, Tilly.'

'Me?' she said.

'And who else would I want to marry but you, Tilly Wilson—the best scone baker this side of the Grampians?' he grinned.

'Oh, get away with you!' she chuckled. 'Come away in. Geordie's in the back bedroom as usual.'

Even a first-year medical student would have known that Geordie Wilson was very ill indeed. Though he smiled a greeting and insisted on shaking Rowan's hand, his face was an unhealthy yellow and his breathing was harsh and laboured. Quickly Rowan made her examination and then glanced across at Ewan with a puzzled frown, but his expression was unreadable.

'Did you bring the pills Geordie needs, Doctor?' Mrs Wilson asked.

Rowan nodded and handed her the two bottles.

'Now I'm sure you'll both not refuse a cup of tea,' Mrs Wilson smiled, leading the way out of the bedroom. 'And I've just taken a fresh batch of scones out of the range, you'll be pleased to hear, Ewan.'

Rowan could hardly contain her anger as she followed Tilly Wilson back into the kitchen. The last thing she wanted was tea. What she wanted to know was why there was no scar on Mr Wilson's thin chest to suggest that he'd undergone surgery, no hair loss to indicate that he'd been treated with chemotherapy.

She made their excuses as soon as was possible and waited only until they were halfway down the track before she grasped Ewan by the arm.

'Is that all the treatment you're giving Geordie Wilson—painkillers?'

He turned to gaze at her, his eyes tired. 'What else would you suggest?'

'My God, if you need me to tell you that, then you've no business to be carrying a stethoscope!' she exclaimed. 'He should be in hospital!'

He looked at her for a moment, his face inscrutable, and then he sighed.

'No amount of surgery or chemotherapy would cure him, Rowan—the cancer's too far advanced.'

'Maybe chemotherapy couldn't cure him but at least it would improve the quality of life he has left,' she protested.

'All right, then,' he said slowly. 'If we hospitalise him and treat him in the way you suggest, how long do you think Geordie will live?'

'I'm a doctor, not a prophet!' she retorted. 'No one can possibly give a prognosis like that.'

'Don't give me specifics, then—just a rough estimate. How long will he live if I send him to hospital?'

She frowned. 'Three—four months,' she said at last.

'Two to three weeks, if we're lucky.'

'Oh, that's rubbish—'

'No, it's not,' he said firmly. 'Geordie's going to die—you know it, I know it and so does Geordie and his wife—but if I send him away from the surroundings and the person he loves most in the world, he'll die a hell of a lot quicker.'

'But you don't know that for sure and it's medically wrong of you to make that kind of decision!' she exclaimed.

He gazed past her at the high hills.

'He came to me when it was too late for me to do anything for him, Rowan,' he said tightly. 'I wish it was otherwise, but it's not. You talk about quality of life—well, in my medical opinion, keeping him at home with the woman he loves and prescribing painkillers is what will suit him best. Perhaps at the Melville they did things differently—'

'Oh, God, you're predictable, aren't you?' she snapped. 'I might have known we'd get round to the Melville eventually—'

'Rowan—shut up.'

'I beg your pardon!' she choked.

'Granted,' he replied with a glimmer of a smile. 'Look, before you tear into me,' he continued as she opened her mouth angrily, 'answer me two questions.'

'But—'

'How many times have you seen Geordie?'

'That's not the point—'

'How many times, Rowan?'

She stared up at him and then away again, and when she spoke her voice was scarcely audible. 'Once.'

'And how long have you known him?'

She gritted her teeth. 'All right, all right, you've made your point. He's your patient, you've known him a lot longer than I have and I've no business criticising your treatment on the strength of one visit.'

'I don't think I could have phrased that better myself,' he smiled.

She sighed. 'OK, get it over with.'

'Get what over with?' he asked.

'You must be itching to give me an earful, so just do it,' she said, her cheeks reddening under his steady gaze.

'Do you want me to?'

'No. . .no, of course I don't,' she faltered. 'It's just. . . well. . .it's just. . .'

'I'm generally so predictable?' he suggested, his eyes warm.

A rueful chuckle came from her. 'I had that one coming, didn't I?'

'No, but I'm afraid I couldn't resist it,' he laughed.

She gazed up at him and as his blue eyes met and held hers she felt a warm glow spreading through her, a glow that she didn't want to feel.

'I'd better go,' she said hurriedly. 'My other patients must be wondering what on earth's happened to me, and I've my clinic this afternoon.'

He nodded and watched her as she walked down to her car, the gold in her hair glinting in the sun.

'You like her, don't you, Ewan?'

He turned to see that Tilly had followed them down the road.

'She might make a halfway decent GP some day if she can learn to stop making snap decisions,' he replied.

'That's not what I meant—and well you know it, lad,' Tilly replied.

A half-smile crossed his face. 'Don't meddle, Tilly.'

'I'm not meddling,' she protested.

'Not yet you're not, but I've seen that look on your face before,' he exclaimed.

Tilly's brown eyes twinkled. 'Why don't you ask her out?'

'What's the point? She won't stay.'

'Like Jenny, you mean?'

His eyes narrowed slightly.

'You wouldn't have lost Jenny if you'd been prepared to move down south and work there,' Tilly continued.

'I won't work anywhere else—you know that.'

She sighed. 'Your mother would never have wanted you to sacrifice your personal happiness like this—'

'That's enough, Tilly!' he interrupted, his voice cold. 'I love you dearly but my private life is my own.'

'So you're not even going to try with Dr Sinclair?' she murmured.

He shook his head.

'She could be different,' Tilly observed. 'She might want to stay if you gave her good reason to.'

'She won't,' he said firmly.

Tilly's thin chest swelled and she pursed her lips in exasperation. 'Well, all I can say, Ewan Moncrieff, is that it's a great pity some of that book learning of yours wasn't married to just a little common sense!'

She wheeled round on her heel and strode away from him, leaving him gazing open-mouthed after her, and then he started to laugh.

He couldn't deny that he was beginning to like Rowan. He had found himself noticing little things about her— like the way she always chewed her lower lip when she was worried, the way the two dimples on her cheeks danced when she was trying hard not to laugh—but he had no intention of getting close to someone whom he suspected would leave the area just as quickly as she had come.

'She's a colleague, that's all,' he said out loud, 'and a damned irritating one at that at times.'

And as the Wilsons' goat bleated its apparent agreement, he laughed again and began to make his way to his car.

*　　*　　*

Laughter was the last thing on Rowan's mind as she drove up to Glen Donan to check the dressings on Fred Johnstone's ulcerated leg, and then called in on the Leonards to examine the new baby.

How was it possible to so thoroughly dislike a man one moment and then to find him extremely attractive the next? she wondered. It wasn't even as though he was her type, she told herself.

She'd always preferred men with blond hair, men who took a pride in their appearance—not men with unruly black hair who looked as though they'd thrown on whatever had come to hand that morning. It made no sense; it made no sense at all.

She shook her head as she parked her car outside Canna's surgery. Get a grip, Rowan, she told herself firmly. You'll be finding the butcher irresistible next, and he's bald, fat and fifty.

'How many have turned up today, Ellie?' she asked as the receptionist came into her consulting-room, carrying some case notes.

'Four. That's one more than last week, and you have to remember it's—'

'It's early days—yes, so you've said before,' Rowan grimaced.

'The posters advertising the clinic haven't been up that long,' Ellie said encouragingly, 'and lots of people only come into the village once a month for their shopping. Once word gets around, the women will start to come— I'm sure they will.'

'Who's first?' Rowan asked, taking the case notes from her.

'Mairi Fisher and her daughter, Beth.'

Ellie's voice spoke volumes but not a muscle moved on Rowan's face.

'Give me a couple of minutes, Ellie, and then show them in,' she said.

Ellie nodded and Rowan waited only until she had

gone before leaning back in her seat with a deep sigh.

It had seemed the easiest thing in the world to set up a clinic specifically aimed at the female population. Even Ewan's cautionary words about the Highlanders' natural reluctance to admit illness hadn't really registered. The Melville had boasted a thriving women's clinic and she had been certain that it could be successfully emulated.

She had been wrong. The young mothers treated her clinic as a baby clinic and the women she really wanted to see—women like Annie Galbraith, who hadn't been near a doctor in years—were noticeable by their absence.

She straightened her shoulders. As Ellie had said, it was early days and she wasn't going to give up just yet, no matter how demoralising it was to spend most of the three hours she had set aside on a Wednesday afternoon waiting for patients who didn't come. Correction, she thought. There were at least two patients who came as regularly as clockwork—Mairi Fisher and her daughter, Beth.

She glanced through Beth's notes, though she virtually knew them by heart now. There was nothing serious, apart from the sheer number of times her mother had brought her to the surgery with ailments that were trivial in the extreme.

'So what seems to be the trouble today, Mrs Fisher?' she asked with an effort as Ellie ushered the mother and daughter in.

'I think Beth's got a bit of a temperature,' Mrs Fisher replied as she sat down. 'I couldn't get her settled last night.'

Rowan nodded and took out her thermometer.

Beth was a pretty, lively, three-year-old with jet-black hair that lay thick and straight round her plump face. She was small for her age, but her bone structure was good and her large brown eyes surveyed the world with a healthy mixture of curiosity and interest. It was quite likely that the child had simply been too full of energy last night to feel like sleeping, but she couldn't be too careful.

'Her temperature's normal, Mrs Fisher,' she declared, 'but I'll just listen to her chest.'

The heart rhythm was perfect, just as she had expected it would be.

'Nothing to worry about there, Mrs Fisher,' she smiled, laying her stethoscope down. 'I think Beth probably just got a bit over-excited last night.'

Mairi nodded.

'And how are you?' Rowan continued, leaning forward in her seat and regarding Mairi thoughtfully. 'Young children can be pretty exhausting—and everyone tends to forget about poor old mum.'

Mairi Fisher smiled weakly. 'I do get tired a lot—but, then, everyone does, don't they?'

Something was wrong, that much was clear. Mairi was only twenty-five and yet she looked as though she had all the cares of the world on her shoulders.

'Is there something worrying you, Mrs Fisher?' she pressed.

Mairi stared at her unhappily, cleared her throat, looked on the point of saying something and then shook her head. 'I'd better not take up any more of your time, Doctor,' she said, getting to her feet hurriedly. 'Thanks for putting my mind at rest—about Beth.'

Rowan sighed. She'd bet money on the real problem being with the mother and not with the daughter, but unless Mairi told her what was wrong she couldn't help her.

'Something wrong?' Matt asked when he came into her room after her clinic had finished and found her lost in thought.

'Frustrating day, that's all,' she answered, getting wearily to her feet.

'Why not let me take you out to dinner—cheer you up?'

'Joan busy tonight, is she?' she smiled.

'Joan was last week,' he said dismissively. 'I'm dating Sarah Urquhart from Auchbain now.'

'Can't you stick with one girl for longer than ten days, Matt Cansdale?' she protested.

'What, and disappoint all the other lovely girls in the area?' he grinned.

She traced a pattern with her finger on the desk. 'If you're free tonight, why don't you ask Ellie out?'

'Ellie?'

'Small, black hair, our receptionist—'

'I know who Ellie is,' he replied, 'but Ellie. . .well. . . Ellie's just Ellie, if you know what I mean.'

'I'm rather afraid I do,' she said ruefully.

'So what about dinner?'

She shook her head. 'Thanks, but no, thanks—I know very well what dinner out with you means!'

'I wouldn't lay a finger on you, I promise,' he said, looking distinctly aggrieved.

'Too right you wouldn't,' she chuckled. 'If you did you'd walk in a very strange way for a fortnight, believe me!'

'Ah, but you're forgetting the female of the species is weaker than the male,' he declared, coming up behind her and grasping her round the waist.

'Like hell she is!' she retorted, twisting round and deliberately bringing her foot down on his.

He let out a yelp of mock pain. 'My God, you've crippled me. . .I'll never walk again!'

'That'll teach you to tangle with the weaker of the species!' she said with a peal of laughter as he stumbled forward, pushing her back across the desk. 'I didn't do self-defence classes for nothing!'

'You're lethal, Rowan Sinclair,' he exclaimed. 'You should have a government health warning stamped on you; you should have—'

'What the hell's going on in here?'

Rowan turned quickly in Matt's arms to find herself staring into a pair of ice-cold blue eyes and a face that was thunderous. It didn't look professional—even she had to concede that—but her clinic was over for the afternoon and there was no need for Ewan to look as though he'd stumbled upon some kind of orgy. Swiftly she extricated herself from Matt's arms, all too annoyingly aware that she was blushing.

'Rowan and I were just fooling about—that's all, Ewan,' Matt declared with a smile.

'Then I suggest you find somewhere else to do it,' he retorted. 'Our equipment might not be new but it's all we've got. I thought you had more sense, Matt.'

'Meaning I have none?' Rowan said, her voice low and her eyes fixed on Ewan's face.

'Meaning whatever you care to have it mean,' he replied steadily.

'Oh, come on, Ewan,' Matt protested. 'Rowan and I—'

'Make yourself scarce, Matt,' she broke in.

'But I'm as much at fault as you are—if fault there is,' he declared.

'Make yourself scarce, Matt,' she repeated, her face white.

He glanced from her to Ewan, then shrugged and went.

Deliberately Rowan picked up her medical bag. 'Well, it didn't take you long to break our agreement, did it, Ewan?' she said with a calmness that was deceptive.

'What did you expect?' he countered. 'When I discover you behaving in a totally unacceptable manner—endangering our equipment—'

'Rubbish!' she said succinctly. 'Nothing has—or would have—happened to your precious equipment. All that Matt and I were doing was having a little fun. I realise you probably find that an alien concept but perhaps if you try to dredge deeply enough down into the recesses of your brain, you might just find you recognise it!'

Hot angry colour spread across Ewan's face. 'That's exactly the kind of flippant remark which demonstrates how unfitting you are to be a country GP!'

'Oh, does it?' she said, her lips a thin white line of anger. 'And is there anything else you'd care to mention whilst you're at it?'

'Yes, yes, there is,' he retorted, nettled. 'Your clothes.'

'What about my clothes?' she asked, her voice dangerous.

'Look at them,' he replied, his eyes scathingly taking in her black leggings and long sweater, emblazoned with the slogan SMILE AND THE WORLD SMILES WITH YOU. 'They're totally unsuitable—'

'Unsuitable for what?' she threw back at him. 'First you disapproved of my London clothes and now you don't like these. What the hell do you suggest I wear— a tweed skirt, cardigan and pearls? Or maybe you'd be happier if I went around in a bin bag!'

'Our patients have a right to expect some kind of standard—'

'Oh, God, must you always be so...so damned stuffy?' she interrupted with exasperation. 'Anyone would think you were eighty years old.' She paused and shook her head. 'No—I take that back—it's insulting to a hell of a lot of eighty-year-olds.'

'We are doctors—'

'Not for twenty-four hours a day, we're not!' she protested. 'We have to let off steam occasionally; we have to do stupid things at times or we'd go completely insane—and then what use would we be to our patients?'

'Rowan—'

'Do you know what's wrong with you?' she said, her voice rising. 'You just can't stand anyone enjoying themselves—that's what's wrong with you! Well, just because you want to go through life being a miserable sod doesn't mean the rest of us have to—and I sure as hell won't!'

She pushed past him and he winced as he heard the

sound of the surgery door banging shut behind her.

'She's got a point, Ewan,' Matt observed as he appeared on the threshold.

'My criticism was justified—'

'Oh, like hell it was!' Matt exclaimed. 'What on earth's got into you lately? You're never off her back—carping, criticising—and she's trying her best to fit in, to do a good job.'

'Are you quite finished?' Ewan said tightly.

Matt stared at him for a moment and then turned on his heel, and did not hear what sounded suspiciously like an oath coming from Ewan's lips as he very unprofessionally kicked the consulting-room door shut.

What the hell was happening to him? he wondered as he threw himself down on her seat. He'd never intended to have a row with her—indeed, when he'd opened her door he'd been feeling quite charitable towards her— and now it had all gone wrong, dreadfully wrong.

He should never have made those remarks about her clothes. There was nothing wrong with her clothes— except that they make you all too aware of her body, a little voice whispered. No, they do not, he thought firmly. I haven't even noticed her body. Oh, no? the little voice continued. Then why wasn't it anger you felt when you opened the consulting-room door and found her in Matt's arms, but jealousy—blind unreasoning jealousy?

'That's rubbish!' he said out loud to the empty room, and heard the little voice whisper mockingly, Is it?

What must she think of him? he wondered, only to groan out loud. She had already made it crystal clear what she thought of him. He'd have to apologise. Why? the irritating little voice demanded. Why should you apologise?

Because I was wrong, because she looked hurt, as well as angry, because. . .because. . . Well, it didn't matter why he felt the need to apologise, he told himself as he strode through the waiting-room past a bemused Ellie and out onto the street—he just knew that he should.

He could hear Rowan's stereo blaring out a raucous dance number even before he reached the stairs leading to her flat, so it was scarcely any wonder that she didn't answer his knock. For a moment he hesitated indecisively outside the door, and then turned the handle.

He hadn't known quite what to expect but it certainly wasn't to find her dancing round the room. She was so obviously enjoying herself and the music was so infectious that, when the song ended and she collapsed breathlessly onto the settee, he couldn't resist breaking into applause, only to see her leap up, red-cheeked, to face him.

'How did you get in?' she demanded.

'I did knock,' he said, 'but you didn't hear me.'

'I was playing the music too loud, you mean?' she retorted. 'Disturbing the neighbours—setting a bad example again?'

He flushed. 'Actually, I was going to say that what you were doing looked like fun.'

'Fun?' she echoed.

He smiled ruefully. 'You were wrong, you know—I do recognise the term.'

She coloured. 'Look, what I said to you. . .I shouldn't have said it. . .but you made me so mad. . .'

'I think I should be the one doing the apologising, don't you?'

She glanced across at him and saw that he was smiling.

'I overreacted and I'm sorry,' he continued.

'But why—?'

'Let's just say I'd had a long day,' he interrupted quickly. 'That record you were dancing to—?'

' "Dance hits of the Nineties"?'

'Put it on again and I'll show you I'm not old before my time.'

'You *dance*?' she exclaimed, unable to hide her surprise.

His face tightened. 'I'm thirty-five, Rowan—hardly pipe and slippers material yet.'

'I didn't mean that,' she exclaimed, acutely embarrassed. 'I just meant I didn't think. . .I mean what I was actually trying to say was. . .'

'Rowan.'

'Yes?' she said awkwardly.

The corners of his mouth lifted. 'Quit while you're ahead—put on the record.'

She shot him a bemused glance and did as he asked.

He was most definitely not at the pipe and slippers stage yet, she decided as the music started and he grasped her hand and whirled her into an energetic dance routine. No mean dancer herself, even she had difficulty keeping up with him, and when the music ended and another song began she held up her hand in protest and leaned against him, struggling to catch her breath.

'Not tired out already, surely?' he chastised, his blue eyes sparkling with triumph.

'Talk about hiding your light under a bushel!' she exclaimed, pushing her damp hair back from her forehead. 'Who taught you to dance like that?'

'A girl called Sophie Williams,' he replied. 'She wanted me to take her to the school Christmas dance and, believe me, you didn't argue with Sophie—not if you actually wanted to see Christmas!'

She began to laugh and as he joined in her laughter he unconsciously drew her closer so that her cheek rested against his, and suddenly she didn't feel like laughing any more.

She could smell the faint aroma of his aftershave and feel his heart beating against hers, but it was the surge of urgent, throbbing longing that flooded through her that caused her to pull back from him sharply, trembling and confused.

'Ready for another dance now?' he asked.

She gazed up at him in confusion. Nothing about him

had changed. The blue eyes, the black hair, the firm jaw—all were the same. Why, then, was she so aware of the feel of his firm warm fingers on her back; why was she so acutely and uncomfortably conscious of his closeness?

'Rowan—is there something wrong?' he asked, his expression perplexed as she stared at him.

She didn't know that her lips had parted slightly, and her eyes had grown softly luminous, but she heard his sudden intake of breath and saw his eyes widen, as though he, too, realised that something had happened.

He moved towards her slightly and, overwhelmingly bewildered by the sensations flooding through her, she put out her hands defensively and saw the glow that had flickered in his eyes for an instant disappear before she could even be certain it had been there.

'I think that's enough dancing for one day,' she said, going over to the stereo to switch it off, her hands trembling.

'Don't want to tire out my old bones, eh?' he said lightly.

'That's the idea,' she said with a laugh that sounded false even to her own ears. 'And I can't be dancing all evening, anyway. I should make a start on my laundry... and then there's the sitting-room... I've bought some paint for it and it isn't going to paint itself...'

Oh, God, she thought, I'm babbling like a schoolgirl. She hadn't felt this unnerved with a man since she was a teenager, and Ewan wasn't helping. He just stood there, staring at her as though she was suddenly a stranger.

'I thought you were on call this evening?' she said, desperately attempting to restore some normality to the situation.

'I am.'

'Then shouldn't...shouldn't you be making tracks?' she suggested.

'There's time enough yet,' he said.

Oh, go, Ewan, her mind screamed, please just go.

'I guess I'd better not keep you back,' he observed at last.

She almost ran to the door to open it.

'Thanks for the dance,' he said awkwardly as he stood on the threshold.

She muttered something incomprehensible in reply and shut the door on him quickly.

This was crazy, totally and completely crazy, she thought as she leant against the door, her heart hammering against her ribcage and her breathing difficult. She didn't want this man—she couldn't want this man. She was still in love with Colin. . .wasn't she?

CHAPTER FOUR

ISHBEL COGHILL's face was white and drawn, her eyes huge with fear.

'I know I should have come to you before, Doctor,' she whispered, 'but I kept on hoping my periods would start again and when they didn't—'

'The absence of your periods—or amenorrhoea, to give it its proper name—could be due to any number of quite ordinary things, Mrs Coghill,' Rowan broke in gently. 'How many periods have you missed?'

'Four. . .maybe five, I'm not sure.'

'And you're thirty-nine, is that right?'

'Thirty-nine in May, Doctor.'

'And you've no family?'

Ishbel shook her head. 'It's not Jim's fault—it's mine. I had endometriosis.'

'It's not a question of fault, Mrs Coghill,' Rowan said firmly. 'No one really knows what causes endometriosis. All we do know is that fragments of the womb lining somehow become stuck to the Fallopian tubes or ovaries. If it's not treated quickly the fragments multiply, causing scarring, and that's what makes it much more difficult for a woman to conceive.'

'When I first went to Dr Ewan to try and find out why I wasn't getting pregnant, he asked if my periods had suddenly become more painful,' Ishbel faltered. 'They had but I thought the pain was normal, so I just ignored it.'

Rowan sighed. 'Sudden, severe period pain isn't ever normal, I'm afraid, Mrs Coghill.'

Ishbel nodded tearfully. 'Do you think. . .my periods stopping. . .do you think I might have a growth, Doctor?

I've noticed some swelling and my aunt, she had a growth—'

'We're not going to know anything until I examine you,' Rowan interrupted quickly. 'So, if you could slip off your clothes—?'

As Ishbel Coghill did as she was asked, Rowan read through her notes quickly. The last time Ishbel had visited the surgery had been five years ago, and while Ewan had noted that he didn't consider it impossible for her to conceive he thought it unlikely. Since then there was nothing, not even a visit to the surgery for a prescription to relieve a bad cold.

She closed the file with a sigh. Ishbel Coghill's amenorrhoea could be due to just about anything—from something quite minor to something very serious indeed. She pulled on her surgical gloves and went to examine her.

'What's wrong with me, Doctor?' Mrs Coghill asked tremulously as she began to pull her clothes back on. 'Is it a growth, a tumour. . .?'

'You're pregnant,' Rowan said with a broad smile. 'That's why your periods have stopped. You're between four and five months pregnant.'

Ishbel sat down limply, her face drained of all colour.

'Are you sure?' she gasped.

'I've letters after my name to prove I should be sure!' Rowan laughed. 'Congratulations.'

'But I can't believe it,' Ishbel said in a daze. 'After all this time, I'm pregnant—I really am pregnant?'

'You really are,' Rowan chuckled. 'Now, I'll arrange for you to have an amniocentesis test—'

'No.'

'It's really a very simple procedure,' Rowan said gently. 'All we do is insert a hollow needle into your uterus to remove a sample of the amniotic fluid—the fluid the baby is suspended in—and neither you nor the baby will feel a thing, I can assure you.'

'No,' Ishbel repeated.

'But it will tell us whether everything is proceeding as it should,' Rowan declared. 'You have to understand that the risks of giving birth to a Down's syndrome child rise the older the mother is, and the amniocentesis test—'

'If the baby isn't. . .isn't perfect, then so be it,' Ishbel declared with determination. 'We'll love him or her just the same.'

'It's your decision, Mrs Coghill,' Rowan said reluctantly. 'All I can say is I'll do my very best to ensure that you and junior sail through the next few months without mishap. It's going to be difficult to say exactly when the baby's due, so I'll book you in provisionally at the maternity unit at the cottage hospital—'

'I want a home birth, Doctor.'

Rowan gazed at Ishbel, appalled. 'Absolutely not!'

'My mother was born at home, I was born at home and I'd like my baby born at home, too.'

Rowan argued, coaxed and cajoled, but Ishbel remained adamant.

'I know you think I'm being foolish, Doctor,' she smiled as she got to her feet, 'but, with you taking care of me, I just know everything will be all right.'

I only wish I was half as confident, Rowan thought as she sat alone in her consulting-room after Ishbel had gone. The only thing she could hope was that eventually common sense would prevail and she would be able to persuade Ishbel to change her mind. It was bad enough that she wouldn't agree to an amniocentesis test, but to want a home birth at her age was madness.

'What on earth did you tell Ishbel?' Ewan asked curiously, coming into her room without warning. 'She's just sailed past me, looking as though you've told her she's won the lottery.'

'She's pregnant.'

'You're sure?'

'Oh, not you, too!' she protested. 'Maybe I should get

my certificates framed and hung on the wall!'

He laughed. 'Well, you've just made one woman's day, that's for sure.'

'I just wish she'd made mine,' she sighed and told him of Ishbel's decision.

'I'd try really hard to talk her out of the home birth if I were you,' he said slowly. 'At her age and with it being her first child. . .'

'The prospect terrifies the living daylights out of me,' she admitted, 'but at least I've got roughly five months to try and change her mind.'

He nodded. The topic of Ishbel Coghill's pregnancy was exhausted, her surgery was over for the day and yet, to her acute discomfort, he showed no inclination to leave.

'Something I can do for you?' she asked as she stacked her case notes into a neat pile.

'It can wait until you're finished,' he answered, perching himself on the edge of her desk.

Determinedly she ignored him, busying herself with tidying her desk and eventually, in desperation, emptying the waste bin.

Since that afternoon in her flat their relationship had undergone a subtle change. He hadn't said anything or done anything—in fact, he seemed as determined to forget about that afternoon as she was—but there had been no more rows and, perversely, she found herself wishing that things could go back to the way they were.

She could cope with his sarcasm and endure his barbed comments, but him being nice all the time was an altogether more unsettling kettle of fish.

'All done now?'

She glanced up at him, pretty sure that she could hear laughter in his voice, but his face was perfectly bland.

'You're free until this evening, aren't you?' he continued.

She nodded.

'I was wondering—if you've nothing planned—whether you'd like to come with me to the cottage hospital?' he suggested. 'I've a patient I want to see and it would give you an opportunity to introduce yourself to the staff there.'

It was a tempting offer but she was not at all sure that she wanted to spend the rest of the day in his company.

'I'll treat you to lunch,' he continued with a smile, sensing her reluctance.

'Lunch?' she exclaimed. 'You and me?'

He looked around him. 'I don't see anyone else I could be inviting, do you?'

She chuckled and then glanced down at her black ski-pants and heavy sweater. 'I'm not really dressed for going anywhere—'

'You look fine,' he insisted. 'So—are you coming?'

Why shouldn't she go? she decided. It wasn't as though he was asking her for a date. All he was suggesting was that she accompany him to Riochan Cottage Hospital as a professional colleague. And what would you have done if he had asked you for a date? a little voice asked. Run a mile, was the distinctly vexing answer. Well, the sooner you get over that particular feeling the better, my girl, she told herself determinedly.

'Of course I'll come,' she declared. 'Just give me a minute to tell Ellie where I'll be in case she needs to contact me.'

The receptionist shook her head in mock despair when she told her where she was going.

'A day off work and you spend it visiting a hospital! Don't you doctors have any imagination?'

Rowan smiled. She supposed Ellie was right. Visiting the cottage hospital would be a bit of a busman's holiday, but though Riochan only carried out minor operations—the more serious cases being sent down to Fort William—there was a maternity ward, geriatric section, and two wards for patients convalescing from major surgery.

It would be interesting to see a cottage hospital in action and it was about time she introduced herself there.

'I take it things are looking up between you and Ewan?' the receptionist observed as Rowan made her way to the door.

'In what way?' she asked and then frowned as a small smile appeared on the girl's lips. 'Forget it, Ellie.'

'Forget what?' she exclaimed innocently, and Rowan scowled and made her way outside, to see Ewan standing next to a very smart Isuzu Truckman.

'What's happened to your car?' she asked in surprise.

'It's in for a service so I've got this on loan for today.'

'Very smart,' she observed as she got in.

'A couple of calls will soon alter that,' he grinned.

'I thought we were just going to the cottage hospital?' she said quickly.

'I've one call to make—out to Frank Shaw's. His daughter suffers very badly from asthma and he's phoned to say that she needs another inhaler. I said I'd drop one in for her. It'll save Matt making a special trip.'

'This Frank Shaw,' she said thoughtfully. 'He doesn't live at Dunscaig, does he?'

He nodded. 'Why do you ask?'

'No particular reason,' she murmured. 'It's just that one of my patients—Alec Mackenzie—works for him.'

'Is there a problem—with Alec, I mean?'

There was, and it was a big one. He had been back at the surgery and she had been shocked at the deterioration in his condition. Luckily he had both looked and felt so ill that she had finally persuaded him to give her a blood sample, but she could not deny that his symptoms had her stumped.

'Look, if there's something you want to discuss, I'm more than willing to listen,' Ewan continued, seeing a slight frown in her eyes.

For a second she was tempted. Another opinion would have been helpful but, though she knew that she was probably just being stubborn, the case was hers, not his, and she desperately wanted to solve it without his help—if only to prove to him that she could.

'There's no need, thanks,' she replied.

He cast her a long sideways look and then shrugged and drew out into the road.

Riochan Cottage Hospital had been built in a spectacular location high above Loch Shiel, but any thoughts of standing to admire the view were quickly lost when they opened their car doors to a biting February wind.

'Snow's on the way, I'd say,' Ewan observed, gazing up at the dark and stormy sky.

'Do you get much normally?' she asked, pulling her sheepskin coat closer to her with a shiver and unwillingly remembering Matt's reference to Mountain Rescue and the practice's commitment to it.

'It depends on the year,' he replied, walking smartly with her across the gravel to the hospital steps, 'but it's usually a fair amount. We're lucky to have got this far through February with none, so perhaps it will be a mild winter this year.'

She fervently hoped that it would be.

'The patient I'm visiting is convalescing in the surgical ward,' Ewan continued, holding open one of the swing doors to let her pass in front of him. 'Do you want to come with me, or would you prefer to go to the staff-room and introduce yourself—there should be one or two members of staff there at this time of day?'

'I'd rather come with you, if you don't mind,' she said.

'I don't mind at all,' he smiled.

The familiar smell of antiseptic hit her nostrils as soon as she stepped inside the hospital and brought back memories of her days at the Melville but there, of course, the similarity ended. The Melville had been carpeted throughout in deep plush Axminster, with a reception area more reminiscent of the foyer of an exclusive hotel than a hospital.

Riochan, by contrast, was typical of a hospital built in the mid 1940s, its flooring dark brown vinyl and its walls clinical white tiles, but though it could never rival the Melville in its appearance the atmosphere seemed a friendly one.

No matter what ward they went into everyone was anxious to meet her and to welcome her to the area, and none was more so than the patient Ewan had come to see—nine-year-old Billy Dean.

'Billy has a fondness for spectacular accidents, don't you, Billy?' Ewan declared, ruffling the child's hair affectionately. 'Tell Dr Rowan what happened to you.'

The child gave a wide, gap-toothed grin. 'I broke my leg, fractured my collar-bone and got internal something-or-others when I fell off the barn roof.'

'You're aiming to be a pilot, are you?' Rowan smiled.

'Inventor,' he replied, his indignant gaze conveying all too clearly that he doubted a mere female would know much about such a subject.

'Billy made his own flying machine,' Ewan explained. 'Unfortunately the superglue proved not to be quite as super as he'd hoped—hence the unscheduled stay in hospital.'

'It was what the books call a. . .a technical hitch,' the child declared.

'I see,' Rowan replied solemnly. 'I bet it gave your mum and dad a fright.'

The boy gazed down at his bed covers. 'I don't have a dad. He was killed in a car crash last year.'

She groaned inwardly, wishing her careless words unsaid, and gazed at Ewan in mute appeal.

'Dr Mitchell reckons you should be fit enough to go back home in another couple of weeks, Billy,' he commented smoothly.

The child sighed. 'He told me.'

'It's not so very long,' Ewan continued with a gentle smile, 'and I brought you something which might help to while away a few hours.'

Curiosity appeared on Billy's face, curiosity that was very quickly superseded by sheer delight as Ewan produced a small but perfectly scaled microscope from his bag.

'This is for me?' he said in awe.

'This is for you,' Ewan confirmed. 'There are some slides to go with it, and a book, too.'

Billy gazed up at him, his small mouth quivering. 'And I can keep it—for ever and ever?'

Rowan's throat tightened as Ewan nodded.

'And now I'm afraid Dr Rowan and I have to be going,' Ewan declared as he got to his feet.

'Can't you stay a bit longer?' Billy protested, catching hold of his hand.

'Not this time, I'm afraid,' he replied. 'But I'll see you again tomorrow.'

'Promise?' the child insisted.

'Promise,' Ewan said firmly.

'You can come again too if you like, Dr Rowan,' Billy observed. 'My mum isn't able to visit very often and you're nice.'

'I think you're very nice, too,' she replied with difficulty.

They left Billy happily examining his microscope but as soon as they were out in the corridor she came to a halt.

'You're visiting him every day, aren't you?' she said.

'It's no big deal,' he said dismissively. 'The journey's a bit difficult and expensive for his mother, that's all.'

'It was kind of you to give him a present,' she continued, her eyes fixed on him.

He couldn't have looked more embarrassed if he'd tried.

'It didn't cost much,' he muttered and made for the stairs, leaving her staring after him.

Why on earth should he be embarrassed at having been discovered doing something kind? she wondered. He was such a strange man. There was so much about him that she didn't know—so much of himself he kept shuttered, closed.

'You're full of surprises, Ewan Moncrieff,' she observed when she'd caught up with him.

'What you see is what you get,' he replied, as they made their way out of the hospital.

'No,' she said thoughtfully. 'There's a whole lot more to you than meets the eye. You know if you'd only lighten up—'

She came to a dead halt. What on earth was she saying? Not only was it extremely insulting, but she also knew only too well that she didn't want him any different. He had to be serious, aloof, for her peace of mind.

'Lighten up?' he echoed, puzzled, and then deep colour swept across his dark face. 'You think I'm dull, don't you?'

'No. . .no,' she said uncomfortably. 'It's just that sometimes. . .sometimes, maybe, you're just a little bit. . .' She put her hands together in mock prayer and gazed heavenwards, her expression a mixture of piety and censure.

He managed to laugh but only just.

Was that really how she saw him, he thought in horror, as some sort of censorious wet blanket? When she'd accused him of being old before his time that day in the surgery he'd thought she was just angry, not that she'd actually meant it.

He didn't used to be dull; he didn't used to be lacking in humour. When he'd been a boy he'd been at the forefront of every practical joke, and when he'd first joined Hugh Fowler's practice there had been time for laughter. When had he changed—why had he changed?

'Sorry. . . What did you say?' he asked in confusion, aware that her eyes were on him.

'I said Mairi Fisher's just gone into the hospital,' she commented with a slight frown.

'So?' he answered with an effort, still stung by her accusation that he was dull. 'She's probably visiting her neighbour—Joyce Belville. She had a hysterectomy last week.'

'Don't you think she comes much too often to the surgery?'

'Beth's her first child and a lot of women are overly protective of their first.'

'Are you sure that's all it is?' she pressed. 'You don't think there's something worrying her—something she's not telling us?'

'The only thing wrong with Mairi Fisher is a fondness for wearing too much perfume and a tendency to worry about her daughter. I've known her since she was a teen-ager, Rowan,' he continued, seeing her uncertainty, 'and I'm sure she'd tell me if there was something bothering her.'

She got into the car with a sigh. He was probably right and she was just seeing problems where there weren't any, and yet she wasn't wholly convinced.

'Where to next?' she asked.

'I promised you lunch, remember,' he answered, 'and I don't know about you but my stomach is beginning to rumble.'

'Lunch it is,' she nodded.

Quickly he drove out of the grounds of Riochan and then took the single track road leading west through the high hills of Glen Darg.

'I've been meaning to ask you how your clinic's going,' he said, pulling momentarily into a passing place to allow the post bus to overtake them.

Pride struggled with honesty within her and honesty won.

'The whole thing's an unmitigated disaster, Ewan,' she sighed.

'The women aren't coming?' he said sympathetically.

She shook her head. 'And if you're about to say, "It takes time"—don't,' she said quickly as he opened his mouth. 'I've heard that so often from Ellie I could scream!'

'It's true, none the less,' he smiled. 'How many clinics have you had—three? There's hardly been time for news of it to reach the country yet.'

'I suppose so, but I thought it would be a lot easier than this. In London women seem much more aware of the value of preventative medicine and the importance of early diagnosis.'

'But you've no regrets—about moving here, I mean?' he asked.

She gazed out of the car window at the hills around her. She'd received a letter from her old boss only that morning, telling her about the changes that were taking place at the Melville and urging her to come back.

He clearly saw her move to the Western Highlands as a brief sabbatical, a temporary holiday, whilst she— What had she seen it as being? A chance to heal her bruised heart, an opportunity to try something different for a while—that was all she'd really seen it as being.

'You're taking an awfully long time to answer, Rowan,' he said thoughtfully.

'Of course I haven't any regrets,' she said briskly and knew that he was not for one moment deceived. 'Why are we stopping here?' she added, as he drew the car to a halt.

'I promised you lunch, remember.'

She gazed out of the car window. There wasn't a hotel or pub in sight and she turned to point that out to him, only to see him extracting two flasks and some plastic beakers from his bag.

'Lunch?' she said faintly.

'Scotch broth and coffee,' he replied. 'What is it— what's wrong?' he added, seeing her lips twitch.

'Boy, but you really know how to spoil a girl, Ewan!' she chuckled.

'You thought I meant lunch at a restaurant,' he said slowly.

'I did, but this is fine,' she insisted, seeing his embarrassed expression. 'There's just one thing,' she added as she stared down into the beaker he was holding out to her. 'You didn't by any chance make this yourself, did you?'

A broad smile lit up his face. 'It's tinned so you're quite safe, I can assure you!'

And she laughed and took the beaker from him.

The soup might have been tinned but on a cold February day, with sleet blowing in the wind, she had to admit that she doubted whether they could have got better in any four-star restaurant.

'That was lovely,' she declared, handing him her empty beaker, and then attempted to clean the windscreen free of condensation, before giving it up as a bad job.

'How are you getting on with Matt?' he asked as he poured her out some coffee.

'Fine,' she said, surprised by his question. 'He's very easy to get on with.'

'Professionally, you mean?'

'Both professionally and personally, I'd say,' she said, puzzled.

He nodded but there was something about his expression that told her he wasn't particularly pleased by her answer.

'Ewan—'

'If I ask you something personal, Rowan, will you give me a straight answer?'

She gazed at him warily. 'It depends upon what it is.'

'An evasive answer if ever I heard one,' he grinned. 'All right, I'll ask my question, anyway. You had excellent career prospects at the Melville. Why did you throw it all away to come to this part of the country where you know no one?'

She stared down into her coffee. She could lie and invent a reason, but somehow it was suddenly important to her that he knew the truth.

'I lived with someone for two years. . . It didn't work out.'

He gazed at her silently and she felt herself colouring.

'Not a very noble reason for taking a job, was it?' she said unsteadily.

To her surprise he smiled. 'Ninety-nine per cent of the people who move north are running away from something—a job they hate, a situation they can't bear any more.' He paused. 'The man you lived with—it's all over now?'

'Oh, yes, it's all over,' she said, but it wasn't over and she knew it wasn't.

Even now, almost a year after Colin had walked out on her, she still caught herself flicking through the mail, half hoping there might be a letter from him; even now, when she lifted the phone she wondered if it could be him calling to say that he was sorry. Travelling six hundred miles hadn't eased her bruised heart and pride at all.

'What happened?' he asked. 'Or would you rather not talk about it?'

'Colin. . . Colin never understood how important my work was to me,' she said, her eyes darkening as she remembered the blazing rows they'd had at the end. 'I guess I can't really blame him—it must be difficult for someone not involved in medicine to understand the commitment it brings.'

'If it's any comfort, it's not necessarily any easier if you're involved with a member of the medical profession,' he observed.

'Like you and Jenny, you mean?'

The words were out of her mouth before she could stop them, and she could have bitten off her tongue at the look on his face. 'I'm sorry,' she said quickly, 'forget I said that—your private life is none of my business.'

'It's OK,' he said with an effort. 'Jenny and I...I guess the main problem was that I can't—won't—compromise.'

She wondered what he wouldn't compromise over but didn't have the nerve to ask and instead laughed shakily.

'We're two fine specimens of the medical profession, aren't we? Paid to help others and we can't even make a success of our own lives.'

'Maybe we just hadn't met the right people.'

Something in his voice made her look up at him and she caught her breath sharply, only to jump at the sound of a peremptory tap on the windscreen.

Quickly Ewan rolled down his window, to find the stern figure of Sergeant Brown of the Canna constabulary standing beside the car.

'Something wrong, Adam?' he asked.

Deep colour appeared on the sergeant's plump cheeks. 'I'm sorry...I didn't realise it was you, Dr Ewan,' he faltered. 'The different car...I thought... What with you being parked here so long and the windows steamed...'

'You thought what, man?' Ewan demanded in confusion as the sergeant subsided into embarrassed silence. 'You're not making any sense.'

'Sorry to have disturbed you, Dr Rowan,' Sergeant Brown continued, snapping to a swift salute. 'Carry on... No, I didn't mean that,' he added, crimsoning still further as he backed away. 'Drive carefully now...there's some ice on the road ahead.'

And with that, he almost ran back to his car.

'What the hell was that all about?' Ewan asked as he turned to face Rowan, only to find her almost doubled up with laughter. 'What is it—what's so funny?'

'He thought...because our car windows were all steamed up...he thought...he thought...'

'He thought what?' he said, puzzled, as another peal of laughter engulfed her.

She wiped her eyes with a shaking hand and struggled

to control herself. 'He thought they were all steamed up because—oh, my heavens—he thought he'd stumbled upon a couple making love!'

'*What?*'

She nodded, as tears of laughter trickled down her face. 'Oh, Ewan, we were on the point of being arrested for lewd and libidinous behaviour in a public place!'

He stared at her, horror-stricken, and then quickly grabbed a duster and began to wipe the windows clean— an action that only sent her into even greater gales of laughter.

'It's not funny, Rowan!' he protested.

'It's priceless!' she choked. 'All your talk about remembering we're pillars of the community. . . Do you realise that if it hadn't been Sergeant Brown, but someone who didn't recognise us, we'd probably be halfway to Canna police station by now?'

'Will you stop laughing?' he demanded, stretching over her to clear her window. 'It isn't funny!'

'Oh, but it is, it is!' she whooped. 'Think about it, Ewan!'

And he probably would have done if he hadn't become aware that in trying to wipe her window clean his arms had somehow enveloped her, and an overwhelming feeling of desire had flooded through him.

'That'll teach you to be a cheapskate,' she chuckled. 'That'll teach you to give me Scotch broth and coffee in the car, instead of taking me to a restaurant. . .'

The rest of what she had been about to say died in her throat, and her laughter faltered as his eyes caught and held hers. He was so close, too close.

'Ewan—'

For an answer he stretched out and captured her chin with his hand. Vaguely she noticed that there was a button missing from his shirt and that one of his cuffs was badly frayed, but what she was most aware of was how blue his eyes were, how strong and yet how gentle his fingers were under her throat and how her own body seemed to be melting instinctively towards him with a will of its own.

She moistened her lips, her throat suddenly dry, but as his lips came slowly down towards her an inner voice whispered warningly, Don't be a fool! and quickly she jerked her head free.

'Hadn't we better be getting on to Frank Shaw's farm?' she said. 'His daughter's inhaler. . .'

Her voice trailed to a halt. She could hardly breathe for the hard hammering of her heart.

'Rowan—'

'You did say it was urgent, didn't you?' she said determinedly, managing to return his gaze—but only just.

Dimly she thought that she heard him sigh as he turned from her and started the car, but her mind was in too much of a turmoil to think rationally about anything. I don't want to feel this way, her mind cried. I don't want to fall in love—falling in love means heartache and pain and I don't want that, not ever again.

They drove in virtual silence to Dunscaig, and when Ewan got out of the car she stayed where she was.

'Don't you want to come in?' he asked.

She shook her head. 'I might just wander around here, get some fresh air.'

He gazed at her indecisively for a moment and then strode off towards the farmhouse, leaving her staring after him.

For a second she debated calling after him, to say. . . to say what? her mind asked. I don't know, I don't know, her heart cried. In fact, I don't seem to know anything very clearly any more. Deliberately she got out of the car, wanting to get as far away from her thoughts as she could, and wandered over to the sheds and barns.

'Afternoon, Doc,' an unfamiliar voice called. 'Fergus Innes,' the man said helpfully when she gazed at him blankly. 'Friend of Alec Mackenzie's?'

Recognition spread across her face. 'I didn't realise you worked here too, Fergus.'

'A year now, Doctor,' he answered. 'Shame about Alec—him not being any better, I mean.'

She nodded.

'I'd better get on,' he apologised. 'Mr Shaw's a stickler for a man doing a full day's work for a full day's pay.'

She smiled and thought that it was a pity Frank Shaw wasn't as much of a stickler about maintaining his farm buildings.

City girl she might be, but even she knew that though the farmhouse was neat and prepossessing the condition of the sheds and barns left a lot to be desired. Doors hung precariously on broken hinges, empty cans had been left where they'd been discarded and there were even some piles of rotting grain lying in corners.

Gingerly she pushed open the door to one of the sheds and found herself in an area the men clearly used for eating their lunch, and yet there was no sign of water to wash with or proper toilet facilities or protective clothing. She sighed. Given such carelessness over simple hygiene and safety, she doubted whether there was even something as basic as a first-aid kit.

She turned to go but a noise in the rafters overhead made her look up, and a shudder ran through her as she saw rats scurrying along. The health and safety people would tear their hair out here, she thought, and it was then that realisation dawned on her.

It couldn't be that simple—or could it? Rats were certainly a carrier of the disease and the flu-like symptoms and constant headaches Alec had been complaining of would fit leptospirosis, but if she was right then Fergus Innes had probably had the disease too and yet Ewan had never said anything.

'You're looking remarkably pleased with yourself,' Ewan said curiously when he returned to the car some time later and found her waiting for him. 'What's up?'

'Could we get back to the surgery as quickly as possible?' she replied. 'There's something I want to check out.'

'Care to tell me about it?' he asked, only to see her shake her head firmly.

'Wait and see,' was all she would say and he shrugged and started the car.

CHAPTER FIVE

A BROAD smile of triumph spread across Rowan's face as she read the report from the Fort William lab.

So she'd been right about Alec Mackenzie—he did have leptospirosis. The disease had come from the rats on Frank Shaw's farm and had probably entered Alec's body through the cuts on his hands. If Frank Shaw had taken better care of the farm, provided protective clothing for his workforce and proper washing facilities, it would never have happened.

As she lifted the phone and dialled the telephone number of the health and safety executive the smile on her face deepened. She'd cracked the case and she hadn't needed Ewan's help. This morning's staff meeting couldn't come too soon.

'OK, are there any more patients either of you want to discuss, or is that the lot?' Ewan asked some time later as she and Matt sat with him round the table in the staff-room.

Rowan cleared her throat. This was her moment and she was going to savour it—the moment when she finally proved to Ewan that she wasn't a passenger but an effective member of the team.

'I've got something to tell you both about Alec Mackenzie,' she declared.

She had their attention now—she could see it—and quickly she explained how she'd discovered what was wrong with Alec, only for her voice to start to falter as dismay appeared on Matt's face and Ewan's mouth tightened into a thin, grim line.

'All right,' she sighed when she had finished and neither of them said a word. 'What have I done wrong now? Should I have told you both before I informed the health and safety—?'

'You shouldn't have brought in the HSE at all, Rowan,' Ewan replied.

'But leptospirosis is a notifiable disease,' she protested. 'Alec definitely has it—'

'And so had Fergus Innes until I treated him with antibiotics.'

'You *knew* Fergus Innes had leptospirosis?' she exclaimed.

'Of course I knew,' he said, running his hand through his hair wearily. 'And I warned Frank Shaw that unless he got his act together I'd phone the HSE. You've put the practice in a hell of a difficult position, Rowan.'

'But how?' she demanded. 'That farm is a disgrace—'

'And the HSE will come down on Frank like a ton of bricks,' Matt observed. 'They could fine him up to £2000, Rowan, and do you really think he'll keep Alec on after that? It's the first job the poor bloke's had in two years.'

'But he could have died!' she exclaimed. 'Leptospirosis can attack vital organs, cause meningitis—'

'And you should have treated him with antibiotics but that's all you should have done,' Ewan interrupted. 'We mustn't get involved in the rights and wrongs of a situation, Rowan, unless it's absolutely essential.'

'Then why didn't you tell me?' she asked angrily. 'You both knew I was treating Alec and I'm not an idiot—I was bound to find out what was wrong with him eventually. If it's anyone's fault it's yours for not telling me!'

As soon as the words were out of her mouth she regretted them. They might be true but Ewan already looked so weary and her words just seemed to add to his fatigue.

'You're right, of course,' he said slowly. 'I should have told you but I forgot for a moment that you were an outsider here.'

She winced.

'All right—maybe I am an outsider here,' she replied, perilously close to tears, 'but I was following the correct procedures—'

'And you always follow the correct procedures, don't you, Rowan?' Ewan broke in, his voice edged with irritation. 'You visit Geordie Wilson once and your first thought is to hospitalise him. You see the Galbraith family once and you're desperate to send in a health visitor or a social worker—oh, yes, you were, I saw it in your face,' he continued as she tried to interrupt.

'This isn't London—this is the country and you can't do things by the book here.'

Angry colour flooded her cheeks. 'OK, I was wrong about Geordie Wilson and the Galbraiths but I'm not a mind-reader, Ewan. If you'd told me about Alec—'

'What's done's done,' he interrupted, getting to his feet. 'There's no point in going over it again.'

'But, Ewan—!'

He didn't wait to hear what she had to say—he just strode out of the staff-room and she turned in desperation to Matt. 'I thought I was doing what was best—'

'I know you did,' he said, patting her shoulder awkwardly. 'I just wish you'd spoken to me or Ewan first.'

It wasn't fair, she thought as she sat alone in the staff-room, it just wasn't fair. She'd been so happy this morning, so pleased with herself, and now it had all gone wrong, horribly wrong.

Tears pricked at the back of her eyes and she blinked them away angrily. How was she supposed to know that in the country phoning the HSE was the last resort, not the first? She had every right to be livid but she wasn't livid. She felt stupid and ignorant and so very much alone.

If only Ewan had yelled at her, but he hadn't yelled at her. He'd simply gazed at her with such disappointment in his face, and somehow that was the worst of all.

The rest of the week was a nightmare.

Alec's wife came down to the surgery and tore her character to shreds in front of a full waiting-room—an attack she had to endure alone for neither Ewan nor Matt had come to her rescue. Being out on call had been even worse. No matter where she went she was sure that people were talking about her, whispering about her, and then, to cap it all, March came in with a blizzard that raged relentlessly for five days.

The one person she hoped to get some sympathy from was Ellie, but even she seemed tense and preoccupied.

'Have you and Matt had some kind of row?' Rowan asked curiously when she eventually managed to corner the receptionist late one morning after surgery. 'Every time I've tried to talk to you he's hanging about looking decidedly sheepish.'

'Is he?' Ellie replied shortly.

'Look, this business with Alec Mackenzie. . . Matt had nothing to do with it.'

'I never thought he had,' Ellie said in surprise.

'So what's wrong—between you and Matt?'

'There's nothing between Matt and me and that's exactly the way I intend to keep it,' Ellie declared, closing the filing cabinet with a bang. 'Now, if we could change the subject, please?'

Rowan gazed at her for a moment and then shook her head. It was none of her business, after all.

'Do you think I'll ever be forgiven, Ellie?' she asked as she stared out of the waiting-room window at the white wonderland beyond.

'In time,' Ellie replied, 'but I'm afraid it's going to take an awfully long time.'

Rowan sighed and watched the snow plough making its tortuous way down the main street.

'Is Ewan giving you a lot of grief over this?' the receptionist continued.

'Actually, he's been very good,' Rowan answered.

So good, in fact, that we haven't exchanged more

than three words all week, she thought miserably.

The phone rang and as Ellie went to answer it Rowan reached for her coat. She might as well go home. There was no point in hanging around the surgery, feeling wretched.

'Wait up there, Rowan!' Ellie called as she dashed back into the surgery. 'That was the Mountain Rescue on the phone. Robbie Galbraith and Peter Henderson have had an accident out on the hills, so I'm afraid your afternoon off's just gone down the tube.'

Rowan gazed at her unseeingly. 'Can't Matt take the call?'

'He's doing the rounds this morning, remember.'

'Then Ewan. . . What about Ewan?'

'He's been on call all night,' Ellie replied. 'Rowan. . . Rowan, are you all right?' she continued anxiously as every vestige of colour drained from Rowan's face. 'What is it. . .what's wrong?'

'I can't do it, Ellie,' she whispered. 'I'm not. . .I'm not very good with heights.'

Ellie stared at her in stunned amazement. 'Why ever didn't you tell us before?' she exclaimed. 'Well, that settles it. . .I'll have to phone Ewan—'

'Don't. . .oh, please, don't,' Rowan begged, grasping the receptionist's arm as she turned to go back to the office. 'He already thinks I'm incompetent and if you have to drag him out of bed to cover for me. . .'

'Be sensible, Rowan,' Ellie protested. 'What else can I do. . .? You can't go. . .'

'Maybe I'll be all right,' Rowan said uncertainly. 'Mountains aren't the same as ladders, are they—they're more sort of sloping? And maybe Peter and Robbie won't have fallen too high up—?'

Ellie shook her head. 'I'm going to phone Ewan.'

'I'll do it, I *have* to do it.'

'But, Rowan—'

'By the time you get Ewan out of bed we'll have

lost vital minutes, Ellie,' she said persuasively. 'I'll manage. . .somehow I'll manage.'

The girl gazed at her indecisively and then hauled a stout anorak and a pair of waterproof trousers from the cupboard behind her.

'If you're going to do this, we'd better have you at least looking the part,' she declared. 'They're Matt's spare set but I'm sure he won't mind if you borrow them. What size boots do you take?'

'A five,' Rowan answered as she dragged on the clothes.

'Thank God we take the same size,' Ellie said, extracting a pair of well-worn boots from her locker. 'Right—let's take a look at you.'

'Will I do?' Rowan asked, rolling up the cuffs of the over-large anorak as best she could and pulling Matt's woollen hat over her curls.

'This is madness—you know that, don't you?' the girl said, worry plain on her face.

'I'll be OK—I *will*,' Rowan declared and made good her escape before Ellie could say anything else.

She knew that what she was doing was insane but the thought of having to face Ewan, of having him know that she had failed again, was just too much. And maybe it wouldn't be too bad, she told herself as she inched her car along the treacherous roads. Maybe, with the snow falling so heavily, she wouldn't be able to see what lay on either side of her.

Any confidence she felt, however, very quickly evaporated as she drew her car to a halt at the rendezvous point and found the Mountain Rescue team waiting for her. They looked so professional, she thought with a sinking heart, whereas she—she felt sick to her stomach.

'Right, Doc, this is the situation,' Joe, the team leader, declared as she joined them. 'Peter Henderson, Robbie Galbraith and Malcolm Dodds went up the hill early this morning. Peter fell, pulling Robbie after him, but

Malcolm managed to get back down to alert us, so we know roughly where they are but not how bad the two lads' injuries are.'

She nodded and tried to look as though she did this every day of the week.

'Robbie's mum's here,' one of the men said in an undertone. 'I think she'd appreciate a word—but make it quick, Doc. We don't want the weather closing in.'

Annie Galbraith was distraught.

'Please. . .oh, please, Dr Rowan, bring Robbie back down safely!' she sobbed. 'I know he's been foolish but I blame myself. I should have stopped his brothers teasing him about his height—that's what's caused this, you see. He's trying to prove himself because he's the smallest.'

Rowan supposed that if she were the youngest of six brothers and a mere five feet ten instead of well over six feet she might feel the need to prove something but why, oh, why, she wondered wretchedly, had Robbie felt the need to prove it this way?

'Doc, I'm sorry but we have to get a move on!' Joe called to her urgently.

Quickly she squeezed Annie's hands and then made her way towards the men, her heart sinking with every step.

'Grand day for a stroll, eh, Doc?' one of them said with a deliberate wink as they set off.

She tried to smile back but all she could think was, Please, God, don't let me make a complete fool of myself. Please, God, don't let me panic and start screaming.

She didn't know how long they climbed—time eventually held no meaning. All she knew was that every part of her body began to scream a protest as she stumbled along in the snow, her head bent low against the icy wind and her breath coming in short, painful gasps. She didn't even feel fear any more, only fatigue—overwhelming, mind-numbing fatigue.

'Over here, Doc!'

'What's happened?' she shouted as she floundered across the snow, scarcely able to keep her balance.

'We've found them—Peter and Robbie!'

She gazed down to where one of the men was pointing and her head spun. Peter and Robbie were on a ledge at least forty feet beneath them.

Quickly the rescue team sprang into their well-rehearsed routine but suddenly she couldn't move. It was as though she was rooted to the spot, paralysed.

'We'll lower you down first, Doc, so you can check on the boys' injuries—Doc—Dr Rowan, did you hear me?'

She glanced up, to find Joe's eyes on her, puzzled, concerned.

'Do I have to go down?' she whispered, her throat so tight that she could hardly speak.

'I reckon diagnosis might be a bit difficult from up here,' he smiled.

She shook her head wildly. 'You don't understand. . .I can't. . .I'm sorry but I can't. . . Heights. . .I can't bear heights.'

His smile died. 'You've picked a hell of a time to tell us that, Doc,' he exclaimed, anger obvious in his face. 'I guess we can manage by ourselves—we've all got first-aid training—but it would have been a hell of a lot better with a qualified doctor.'

Not with some stupid woman who's just gone to pieces, she added for him mentally, all too unwillingly remembering what Ewan had said to her the first night they'd met.

She clenched her hands together. 'Lower me down.'

'But, Dr Rowan—'

'Lower me down,' she repeated determinedly.

He stared at her uncertainly and then gave the order.

Everything happened very fast after that. She kept her eyes shut tightly when they lowered her down to the ledge, but when she reached Peter and Robbie her professional instincts took over. Peter had a fractured shoulder-blade and Robbie a broken leg, and they were both suffering from the early stages of hypothermia. Quickly she applied splints and then tugged on the rope for the stretcher to come down.

'The boys have to go up first—you understand that, don't you, Doc?' one of the team said as they carefully eased Peter onto a stretcher.

She swallowed hard. 'Don't worry about me—I'm all right—just concentrate on the boys.'

The stretcher swung dizzily for a second in front of her eyes and then was gone. Concentrate on Robbie, she told herself. Don't look down. Concentrate on Robbie and you'll be all right.

'Holding in there, are you, Doc?' Joe asked, his gaze anxious as he came down with another stretcher for Robbie.

'Never felt better,' she said shakily.

'You're doing great,' he smiled. 'Won't be long now and you'll be back with the rest of us.'

She nodded but as he disappeared with Robbie on the stretcher panic began to creep over her. The wind had changed. It was coming in great squally, snow-filled gusts from the east. It wouldn't be an easy ascent, even she knew that.

'Your turn now, Doc!' someone shouted from above and gingerly she pulled on her rope in answer.

Her ascent seemed endless. Time and time again she was buffeted against the rock face and once she felt a searing pain shooting through her leg, but all she could think of was hold on—hold on though her back ached and her arms felt as though they were being torn from their sockets—hold on and she'd be all right.

'Well done, Doc!' Joe beamed when she reached the ridge. 'For a girl who's frightened of heights you've done bloody marvellously!'

'I did it!' she said, feeling quite extraordinarily

elated. 'I can't believe it, but I actually did it!'

'We've still got to get back down,' he reminded her.

'Easy as falling off a log,' she beamed.

'You've hurt yourself,' he declared suddenly.

She followed the direction of his gaze. Both her protective trousers and the ski-pants she had on underneath had been ripped through and blood was pouring from an ugly gash on her leg.

'It looks nasty,' he observed. 'Will you be able to make it down—we've a spare stretcher—?'

'Not on your life!' she exclaimed, pulling an absorbent pad from her bag. 'If you think I'm going to be carried down the hill you can forget it!'

'Good on you!' he grinned.

The descent down the hill was hard but sheer adrenalin kept Rowan going to the rendezvous point, where an ambulance was waiting.

'Thank you, Doctor, oh, thank you,' Annie Galbraith said fervently. 'I don't know how I'll ever be able to thank you!'

'How about coming in for your cervical smear examination?' Rowan said. 'I've sent you three invitations and you haven't turned up for one of them.'

Mrs Galbraith flushed to the roots of her red hair.

'It's a question of finding the time, Doctor, and what with the roads being bad—'

'They weren't that bad last Friday, Annie.'

'I'll make an appointment some time,' Annie muttered, edging her way towards the ambulance. 'I'll come in some time, I promise.'

She wouldn't come in—Rowan knew for certain that she wouldn't come in and she closed her eyes in defeat. Now that the excitement was over her leg had started to throb quite badly, but her main feeling was that of anger.

What did she have to do to persuade women like Mrs Galbraith to come forward for a simple examination that could save their lives? She could have been killed this morning and yet still she could not convince Annie of the value of preventative medicine.

'I'd get that leg of yours seen to, if I were you, Doc,' Joe observed as he began to stow his gear into the back of one of the Land Rovers.

'I will,' she answered.

'And the boys would like you to know you can come out with us any time,' he continued.

'Maybe I should take a few lessons first,' she laughed and didn't see Ewan's Land Rover sliding to a halt behind her.

He'd driven like a madman from Canna, dreading what he would find after Ellie had phoned him in panic, and the relief he felt at finding Rowan alive was overwhelming— overwhelming but short-lived.

How dared she stand there, looking as though she'd been out for a Sunday stroll, he thought furiously, when he'd been to hell and back, imagining her slender body lying broken and bleeding at the bottom of a cliff? How dared she laugh with the rescue team when all he'd been thinking was that if she was dead he'd never have the chance to tell her—? To tell her what? a little voice asked, and he didn't like the answer he got one bit.

Deliberately he strode up to her and spun her round, only to see a wide smile on her face—a smile that merely incensed him further.

'Ewan!'

'Don't you possess an ounce of bloody sense in your entire body?'

'Wh-what?' she stammered, the smile on her lips dying.

'Just what the hell did you think you were doing going out with the Mountain Rescue when you're frightened of heights?' he thundered, his face white. 'If you didn't think of yourself, couldn't you have spared a thought for the rest of the team and the patients? Someone could have been killed this morning because of your stupid heroics!'

'We all got down safely,' she said defensively, 'and Joe said I did a good job—'

'Can you do *nothing* right?' he continued as though she hadn't spoken. 'First it was Alec Mackenzie and now this! Do you think I enjoy being dragged out of my bed to rescue someone who should have known better?'

'I didn't need rescuing!' she protested. 'You didn't have to come. . .I didn't ask you to come. . .'

And suddenly it was all too much for her. Alec Mackenzie, the terror she had felt on the hill, the injustice of his criticism when she had only been trying her best— to her horror, hot tears began to trickle down her cheeks. She tried to stop them, dashing a shaking hand across her face, but it was no use—more just came.

'Will you stop. . .shouting at me?' she cried. 'You're always. . .shouting at me and I've had enough. . . I've just had enough. Nothing I do is right; nothing I say is right. I try my best and you. . .you just shout at me!'

He stared at her, aghast. 'Rowan—'

'You're a bully!' she wailed, all too conscious of the embarrassed faces of the Mountain Rescue team and that she was sounding like a child, but unable to help it. 'You're nothing but. . .but a big bully!'

'Rowan. . .*don't*. . . oh, please, don't cry,' he began, taking a step towards her, only to see her back away.

'Go on. . .say it,' she hiccuped. 'Say it. . . Typical female reaction. . .bursting into tears when things get rough. Well, you can say what you damn well like as far as I'm concerned because I've had it with this job and I've had it with you. You were right. . . Are you happy to hear that? I can't cope. I thought I could, but I can't. . .I can't!'

Appalled horror appeared on his face and he caught her hands in his.

'Rowan, oh, Rowan, I'm sorry. I know I have a sharp tongue but I never meant to make you cry!'

She pulled her hands from his, her face paper-white and her grey eyes huge with strain.

'Get. . .get stuffed!' she said and then, with as much dignity as she could muster, she began to limp her way to her car, only to feel herself restrained by two firm hands.

'You've hurt yourself—'

'Next time I'll try to break my neck,' she sniffed. 'That should make you happy.'

'Where are you hurt?' he demanded.

'Does it matter?' she replied, trying to wrench her hands free without success.

'She's got a bad cut on her leg, Ewan,' Joe declared. 'When we were pulling her up she must have hit some rocks.'

Firmly but gently Ewan led her across to his car. 'Did you hit your head at all?' he said, forcing her to sit down.

'No. . .at least. . .no, I don't think so,' she answered, gripping her bottom lip between her teeth as he pulled aside the torn edges of her trousers and touched the wound gently.

'Do you feel giddy, or sick?'

'No,' she murmured.

Quickly he took his ophthalmoscope out of his bag.

'This isn't necessary, Ewan—'

'Shut up and look over my left shoulder.'

She did as he asked.

'No sign of brain damage, then?' she said with a small smile when he put his ophthalmoscope back into his bag.

'With you, it's a bit difficult to tell,' he said without rancour. 'Now, apart from your leg, have you any pain anywhere else?'

She shook her head. 'I reckon I could do the Highland fling for you, if you want.'

'Don't make promises you undoubtedly couldn't keep,' he smiled, some of the tension in his face lifting. 'OK, I'll just have a word with the boys and then we'll get you down to the surgery, where I can give you a full examination.'

'*No!*'

Ewan and half the Mountain Rescue team turned in unison, their faces registering varying degrees of surprise.

'I don't need to be examined,' Rowan continued determinedly. 'There's nothing wrong with me but a cut on my leg. You can stitch it if you like but that's all you need to do.'

Ewan's jaw set. 'Since when did you develop X-ray vision? You could have dislocated a shoulder, have internal injuries—'

'That's right—look on the bright side,' she interrupted with a watery smile, but he refused to be placated.

'Why won't you let me examine you?' he demanded. 'At the very least I can confirm your rough and ready diagnosis.'

She shook her head. 'I'm a doctor too, remember, and I think I'd know if I'd really hurt myself badly.'

He gazed at her with frustrated anger and she knew that she was being foolish but the thought of taking her clothes off for him and of having his hands touch her bare body—even for a medical examination—was too unnerving.

He sighed in defeat.

'All right, have it your own way, but I'm definitely putting stitches in that cut. God alone knows how much blood you've lost, and I'll not have you bleed to death just because you're too damn stubborn to let me treat you!'

It took an age to reach Canna—the road conditions saw to that—but as Ewan slowed outside the surgery she grasped his hand quickly.

'Couldn't you do the stitches at my flat? Please, Ewan,' she continued as he opened his mouth to protest. 'Matt and Ellie will probably be in the surgery—'

'And you can't face an inquisition?' he finished for her. 'OK, your place it is.'

She managed to get out of his car without too much difficulty, but when she reached the staircase leading to her flat she paused. Suddenly there seemed to be an awful lot of steps.

'Something wrong?' he said quickly. 'Are you in pain?'

'No. . . Just give me a couple of minutes. . .'

'That settles it,' he declared and, before she knew what he was doing, he had swept her up in his arms.

'What do you think you're doing?' she protested.

'Getting you up to your flat the easy way,' he said. 'If you prefer, I can put you down and let you crawl up—it's up to you.'

He waited and eventually she nodded.

'You know it must be bloody marvellous,' she muttered into his chest as he began to climb the stairs.

'What must be?' he asked.

'Always being so damned right about everything!' she exclaimed.

He laughed deeply and rested his chin on the top of her head, conscious of how right it felt there and how sweet her perfume was.

'If I'm too heavy, you can put me down,' she murmured, conscious that he had paused.

'No, you're not too heavy,' he said with difficulty, and deliberately quickened his stride.

'Thanks for the lift,' she said when he'd sat her down on a chair.

'Any time,' he said briskly. 'Now, we'd better get you out of those clothes—'

'I can manage,' she said hurriedly, easing herself out of the bulky anorak and pulling off her waterproof trousers.

'Shouldn't you take off your other trousers too?' he said as he pulled a chair over and sat down in front of her. 'If you keep them on I'll have to cut them—'

'They're ruined, anyway,' she answered, fighting with her mounting colour.

There was no way that she was going to take off her ski-pants for him and sit there in her knickers—no way.

He shrugged and, taking a pair of scissors, cut her ski-pants to the knee and then took a syringe from his bag.

'I'm afraid this is going to hurt a little,' he commented as he administered the local anaesthetic to her leg.

She drew in her breath sharply.

'That's one lie I'm never going to tell a patient again,' she murmured. 'It doesn't hurt a little—it hurts like hell!'

He grinned. 'Just be grateful you hurt your leg and not your face. You're going to be left with a biggish scar, no matter how careful I am.'

She couldn't resist it. 'Damn.'

'Why "damn"?' he asked. 'I shouldn't think anyone will notice too much.'

'Matt will.'

'What makes you say that?' he asked with studied casualness, pressing the skin around her leg to see if it was numb.

'Because you told me once that the first thing Matt notices about a woman is her legs.'

'When did I say that?' he asked, puzzled.

Her eyes sparkled. 'When you said he'd employ a trained chimp if her legs were good enough.'

He flushed. 'I say too damn much at times. Now try and keep as still as you can,' he continued. 'This stitching's going to be tricky, so I don't want another word out of you unless you feel any pain.'

As his left hand cupped her leg to steady it she sat motionless, trying to divorce herself from the situation and ignore the sensations his hands and his nearness were awakening in her, but it was a relief when he started to clear away his soiled swabs.

'Will I live, then?' she said as lightly as she could.

He didn't answer. He just knelt there, gazing at her, and then reached out and cupped her face in his hands.

She didn't move, didn't say a word—she just gazed back at him, her heart in her mouth. She could see herself mirrored in his eyes, could hear that his breathing was as ragged as hers, and then slowly, very slowly, his lips came down on hers.

She didn't pull away as he deepened the kiss—as his tongue gently explored her mouth. All she was aware of was the shudder of expectation that ran through her body, of the desire to have him nearer, nearer. He was holding her as though she were made of glass and it was she who pulled him closer, running her hands up his rough tweed jacket to the nape of his neck and locking her fingers there.

Dimly she heard him groan and she sighed as his lips left her mouth to tease the fluttering pulse at her throat with his tongue. Never before had a man seemed to know exactly what chords to strike in her. Never before had her breasts ached to be released from the confines of her bra—to have a man's hands touch them, his mouth taste them.

All her resistance seemed to be crumbling, disintegrating under the magic touch of his hands and lips. And then she remembered—she remembered all too vividly that she had wanted Colin once and he had torn her heart apart.

'I'm sorry,' she gasped as she pulled herself free from his arms. 'I'm so sorry but I can't. . .I just can't.'

'What is it, what's wrong?' he asked in confusion.

'It isn't you,' she faltered. 'Please don't think it's you. . . It's me. I. . .I like you very much but. . .'

'You're still in love with Colin?' he sighed, leaning back on his heels.

'No. . .yes. . .oh, I don't know,' she murmured, her eyes clouding. 'All I do know is that I don't want to be hurt again.'

'Oh, lass, I'd never hurt you,' he said softly, his blue eyes full of compassion.

'I don't think you'd mean to,' she said, her voice low, 'but Colin. . .he said he loved me and then when he left. . .'

'You decided you'd become a nun for the rest of your life?'

'That isn't fair, Ewan,' she whispered, her face strained.

'I'm sorry,' he said ruefully, 'but, Rowan, I think I'm falling—'

She put her fingers to his lips quickly to silence him and he smiled.

'All right, lass. I won't say another word—I'm a patient man—I can wait.'

She gazed up at him, seeing the kind concern in his face, and then looked away quickly, her heart thudding against her ribs. She wanted him—she knew she did—but she was so afraid, so afraid.

'I want you to get some sleep now,' he said, getting to his feet, 'and you're to take the next ten days off.'

'I don't need—'

'Doctor's orders,' he said firmly, and then kissed her hair lightly. 'You're too special to lose, lass.'

She didn't say a word—she couldn't. She just waited until she heard the sound of his feet disappearing into the distance on the stairs outside and then put her head on her arms and sobbed as though her heart would break.

CHAPTER SIX

'YOUR blood pressure's gone up, Ishbel.' Rowan frowned as she stared at the pressure gauge. 'You've been overdoing it again, haven't you?'

'I haven't,' she protested. 'I've been taking things easy like you said, leaving most of the work on the croft to Jim—'

'So that you could run round Fort William, choosing wallpaper for the nursery and baby clothes.'

'I haven't!'

Rowan gazed at her severely. 'You were seen, Ishbel.'

Ishbel scowled. 'It was Mrs Ross who told you, wasn't it? That nosy, interfering—'

'Actually, it was Ellie,' Rowan laughed. 'She was in Fort William, choosing a dress for the ceilidh next Thursday, and she saw you.'

'I didn't go into that many shops, Doctor—'

'You shouldn't have been in Fort William at all,' Rowan declared. 'You're seven and a half months pregnant—'

'And I'm an older first-time mother—yes, I know, you've told me all that before.'

'Then why don't you listen to me?' Rowan exclaimed vexedly. 'Look, I'm warning you, Ishbel, if your blood pressure keeps on see-sawing like this I'll hospitalise you for the rest of your pregnancy. I mean it,' she added as Ishbel frowned. 'If I find out you've been down to Fort William again I'll ground you!'

Ishbel nodded and left the consulting-room with a sigh, not seeing the smile that crossed Rowan's face.

She supposed that she would have been the same if she'd been in Ishbel's shoes, but the quieter and calmer she could keep her for the next few weeks the better it would be for her own peace of mind.

'Nothing wrong with Ishbel, is there?' Ewan asked as he brought in her mail. 'She looked really down when she passed me.'

'I've just clipped her wings,' she chuckled. 'She's OK, really,' she added as his eyebrows rose. 'Her blood pressure's a bit high, that's all.'

'You're getting really involved, aren't you?' he observed.

'I know I shouldn't be,' she admitted, 'but Ishbel was so happy when I diagnosed her pregnancy and I just want everything to go well for her.'

'You've still not managed to persuade her to have her baby at Riochan?' he commented.

She shook her head. 'I'm still working on it, believe me.'

'Well if anyone can wear her down, you can,' he declared as he made for the door. 'You're the most cussed female I know.'

She gazed at his retreating back for a moment and then deliberately stuck out her tongue.

'I know exactly what you're doing, Rowan Sinclair,' he observed, without turning round, 'and all I can say is it's childish, very childish!'

A peal of laughter rang out behind him and a broad grin lit up his face, a grin that lasted only until he reached the crowded waiting-room and found himself in the middle of what looked like a full-scale row.

'What's going on, Ellie?' he asked, gazing from her flushed face to Alec Mackenzie's stormy one.

'I'm trying to explain to Alec that if he won't see Dr Rowan he's going to have to wait until Wednesday for an appointment with you.'

'What's this all about, Alec?' Ewan demanded.

'I won't have that woman treating me or my family,' he replied, his cheeks red but his gaze defiant.

Ewan's eyebrows snapped down. 'Get Dr Rowan for me, Ellie.'

'She's already late for the morning rounds—'

'*Now*, Ellie.'

She took one look at his face and disappeared, leaving a ripple of whispered comment running round the waiting-room.

'I have a perfect right to choose which doctor I see,' Alec declared, tugging at his collar nervously.

'Indeed you do,' Ewan replied, his voice even.

'You can't make me see that woman,' Alec continued belligerently, only to lapse into silence as Rowan appeared in the doorway.

'Something wrong?' she asked, gazing uncertainly from Ewan's tight face to Alec's red one.

'Right, Alec,' Ewan said with a calmness that was unnerving, 'I want you—all of you,' he added, gazing round the uncomfortable faces in the waiting-room, 'to listen to me and to listen good. "That Woman" has a name, Alec, and you will use it. You will refer to her as Dr Rowan or Dr Sinclair—nothing else, do you hear me?'

Alec's colour deepened perceptibly but he nodded.

'Dr Rowan made a mistake when she contacted the HSE,' Ewan continued. 'All right, it was a big one,' he added as Alec opened his mouth, 'but her actions were motivated by the best of intentions.'

'She lost me my job!'

'*She?*' Ewan said dangerously.

'Dr Rowan,' Alec mumbled. 'Dr Rowan lost me my job.'

'You might also care to remember that Dr Rowan probably saved your life,' Ewan observed. 'If you no longer wish to be treated by her that's your prerogative, but I have to say I also think it's your loss. I would have no hesitation in putting my life in Dr Rowan's hands any time.'

Alec opened his mouth, clearly thought the better of what he'd been about to say and slammed out of the surgery, leaving a stunned waiting-room behind him.

'That should give them all something to talk about for the rest of the day,' Ewan chuckled as he followed her along to her room.

'Did you really mean that?' she asked. 'About trusting me with your life?'

'I wouldn't have said it otherwise,' he replied. 'Look, you made a mistake but it's high time this particular chapter was closed. I don't think Alec will ever willingly see you as a patient again, but he's only one man and you've made a lot of friends here.'

'The most important one being you, I think,' she smiled, only to see him grimace.

'I was rather hoping you saw me as something more than just a friend, Rowan.'

She stared down at her desk. 'Don't. . .don't rush me, Ewan.'

'I won't, lass,' he murmured, tracing the contours of her cheek with his finger, 'but it's hard to be patient when you keep on getting prettier every day. And now you'd better get going before our patients start sending out a search party for you,' he added with an effort.

She nodded but she was still standing lost in thought several minutes later when Ellie came in to collect her files.

Ellie eyed her thoughtfully.

'Look, I know it's none of my business,' she said, 'but Ewan. . .he's a nice man.'

'I know.'

'So what's the problem?'

The problem is that I like him very much, Rowan thought, but then I liked Colin a lot too before it all went sour.

'Rowan—'

'I'd better go, Ellie,' she said and headed quickly for her car.

It was a long and tiring day. By the time she had called on five patients in Glen Donan and then travelled all the way up to Glen Eillan to discover that, far from being at death's door, Ian Norris was out on his tractor with nothing more serious than a head cold, she was longing to go home and yet she still had to call in on Geordie Wilson.

Every time she visited Geordie it was to find him a little more frail, a little more shrunken. Ewan was prescribing stronger and stronger dosages of morphine and she knew that it was only a question of time before Geordie's wasted frame could tolerate no more, and yet Tilly was still maintaining a cheerful, positive attitude— an attitude Rowan was finding increasingly difficult to share.

It was with relief, therefore, as well as surprise, that she saw Ewan's Land Rover parked outside the Wilsons' croft as she drove up the rough track to the house.

'Afternoon, Dr Rowan,' Tilly beamed as she came out to meet her. 'It's a grand April day, if a bit cold.'

'How's Geordie today?' Rowan asked with a brightness she was very far from feeling.

'Fair to middling,' Tilly answered. 'Come away in— I baked simnel cake this morning as it's almost Easter.'

'I see Dr Ewan's here,' Rowan commented as she followed her.

Tilly nodded. 'He'll not keep away, though I've told him time and time again he owes us nothing. When we took him in after his mother died it was for our sakes as much as his own, for we'd no bairns of our own and he'd always been a good lad.'

'I didn't know you looked after him when his mother died,' Rowan said in surprise.

'He keeps too much to himself, does Ewan,' Tilly sighed. 'If I were to tell you only half—'

She came to an abrupt halt as Ewan came out of her husband's bedroom.

'I'm not interfering, I can assure you, Rowan,' he said quickly as soon as he saw her. 'It's just—'

'I know why you're here,' she broke in, 'and I understand.'

He gazed at her curiously, and she quickly went through to the bedroom to examine Geordie.

'Everything all right, Doctor?' Tilly asked when she returned to the sitting-room some time later.

Geordie Wilson was never going to be 'all right' and she was finding it harder and harder to pretend that he would be, but under Tilly's anxious gaze she found herself nodding.

'You'll be going to the ceilidh next week, Dr Rowan?' Tilly continued, as she handed her a cup of tea and a slice of the simnel cake. 'Geordie and I never missed one when we were younger.'

'I'm afraid I'll have to give it a miss,' Rowan answered. 'I'm on call that night.'

'But you have those mobile phone things now, don't you?' Tilly protested. 'If anyone needed you they could contact you easily.'

'Perhaps,' Rowan smiled, 'but I don't drink, you see—'

Tilly shook her head. 'It's easy seeing you're a Sassenach. People from down south always think a ceilidh means nothing more than some dancing and a lot of drinking. If it's a proper ceilidh there's conversation, singing, a little dancing—'

'And a lot of drinking,' Ewan finished for her with a grin.

'Ewan's going, aren't you, lad?' Tilly said thoughtfully. 'Why don't you go together—you'd be company for one another.'

A faint flush of colour appeared on Rowan's cheeks. 'My leg's not really up to much dancing yet, so I'll probably just give it a miss. And now I really have to be going,' she added as Tilly opened her mouth, clearly intending to protest. 'I'm doing evening surgery tonight.'

'You should take better care of this girl, Ewan,' Tilly commented reprovingly as they accompanied Rowan to the door. 'She's looking fair done.'

'She means you're looking tired,' Ewan chuckled, seeing Rowan's puzzled expression, 'and I'm afraid no one tells this girl anything, Tilly. She was supposed to take ten days off work after her accident but she was back at work in five!'

'Another workaholic!' Tilly said with a shake of her head, and Rowan smiled and said nothing.

How could she say that the real reason she'd gone back to work so quickly was because she couldn't bear sitting alone in her flat? It gave her too much time to think—too much time to remember the sensations that Ewan's touch had awakened in her.

As they stood on the doorstep, however, Rowan cleared her throat awkwardly. There was something she knew she had to say, no matter how upsetting it might be for Tilly Wilson to hear.

'Tilly. . . Tilly, you do know, don't you, that if things start to become. . .difficult for you we could arrange for your husband to go into hospital?' she said gently.

'We've no' been separated all the years we've been wed, Doctor, and we'll no' be parted now,' she replied.

'But you're not strong yourself and. . .' Rowan reached out and took one of Tilly's tiny hands in hers. 'You do know that Geordie hasn't much time left, don't you?'

'Of course I know it—we both do,' Tilly replied, her eyes shimmering, 'but we've had many happy years together and we're no' feared of death. I'll grieve for him when he goes because I'll no' be able to see him but I know he'll be there, waiting for me on the other side.'

Rowan gazed at her unseeingly, her throat tight.

'He'll stay until until the daffodils come,' Tilly continued, her kindly brown eyes fixed on Rowan's face. 'He was always fond of the daffodils.'

'The daffodils?' Rowan echoed.

'When Geordie and Tilly were first married she wanted a garden but the ground is poor, as you can see,' Ewan explained. 'Geordie wouldn't be beaten, though. He went to Fort William and came home on the train with plants and bushes.'

'I tended them and watered them,' Tilly declared with a reminiscent smile, 'but come the winter they all died— all but the daffodils. Each year they multiplied until now, at the end of April, it's just one huge golden carpet out there.'

Rowan stared at the patch of ground in front of the house. There were a lot of green leaves, certainly, but it didn't look as though anything much would flourish in that dark, inhospitable earth.

'They will come, Doctor,' Tilly said, seeing the direction of her gaze. 'They're strong things and they will come—they always do. Geordie says they remind him of me.'

'Of you?' Rowan said, her voice husky.

'Beautiful things living in a harsh environment,' Tilly chuckled. 'He's a daft, romantic beggar at times is Geordie. He'll stay with me until the daffodils come, Doctor, and then he'll go.'

Out of the corner of her eye Rowan saw Ewan move away, but not before she'd seen his face twist with pain, and with a murmured farewell to Tilly she followed him.

'Why didn't you tell me Geordie and Tilly took care of you when your mother died?' she asked softly. 'When I think of what I said to you—virtually accused you of negligence in your treatment of him. Why didn't you tell me that you knew what was best for him because you loved him?'

'Because the only way I can cope with this is to keep telling myself he's a patient,' he said tightly.

'But he isn't just a patient, is he?' she pressed.

He took an uneven breath. 'Leave it, Rowan. . .I know you mean well but please. . .please just leave it.'

'Oh, Ewan, you're not a machine, however much you like to pretend you are,' she protested. 'You're just an ordinary man who happens to be a doctor. It isn't wrong to care; it isn't wrong to feel; it isn't wrong to hurt.'

'You'd better go or you'll be late for surgery,' he said, his face shuttered, closed.

She put her hand on his arm, wanting to comfort him, only to feel it shrugged off.

'Go, Rowan,' he said, his voice thick. 'Please. . .please just go!'

And she did, but she drove back to Canna with tears welling in her eyes for a man who was hurting so much and who wouldn't let her help him.

Evening surgery did little to lift her spirits. The snows of early March had given way to a wet and windy April and the number of patients suffering from simple colds and flu had multiplied accordingly. Only one bright moment relieved the endless stream of coughing, sniffing patients and that was the arrival of Robbie Galbraith and his five brothers.

'Robbie has something he'd like to say to you, Doctor,' the eldest of the brothers announced, deliberately digging his elbow into his young brother's ribs.

'I'm very grateful to you for getting me down from the hills, Doctor—especially since we've found out you're feared of heights,' Robbie declared in the carefully measured tones of a man who had been rehearsing his speech for days. 'What I did was stupid and thoughtless, but. . .' He paused and glanced at his brothers quickly. 'But it would have been some achievement if I could have pulled it off!'

That this was not part of the rehearsed speech was obvious as five pairs of Galbraith eyebrows snapped down reprovingly.

'How's the leg, Robbie?' she asked, deliberately changing the subject.

'Blood—very itchy,' he corrected himself quickly, gazing down with annoyance at his heavily plastered leg.

'Think yourself lucky that's all you broke,' she smiled.

As she watched them go, ramrod stiff in their best Sunday clothes, she could not help but remember how disparaging and critical she'd been of the family when she'd first arrived.

Four months of working in the area had changed all that. The Galbraiths did not possess much in monetary terms, and their home was a chaotic mess, but they had something that all the money and the orderliness in the world couldn't buy—love and laughter.

The Western Highlands and its people had taught her much during her stay here and the most important of those teachings had been not to make snap decisions about anything or anyone.

'Haven't you got a home to go to?' Matt protested when he came into her room long after evening surgery had finished and found her hard at work on her files.

'I shan't be much longer,' she replied. 'I just want to finish this.'

He shook his head. 'It's high time you got yourself a social life.'

'Good night, Matt,' she said firmly, but he didn't go away. He just stood there, looking distinctly ill at ease.

'Something I can help you with?' she asked.

'I need a favour.'

She put down her pen and eyed him suspiciously. 'What kind of a favour?'

'I want you to speak to Ellie for me.'

She gazed at him in confusion, only to see a deep flush of colour appear on his cheeks.

'All right, Matt, what have you done to upset her?' she sighed. 'I've noticed the two of you are hardly speaking—'

'I haven't done anything to upset her,' he protested. 'Well, not intentionally, anyway. The thing is. . .the thing is she won't go out with me and I thought maybe if you had a word—'

'Forget it, Matt,' she declared. 'There's no way I'm getting involved in your tortuous love life.'

'All I want is for you to put in a good word for me,' he explained. 'Ellie seems to have this impression that I'm some sort of rampant Casanova, you see.'

'Now how could she possibly have got hold of that idea?' Rowan said drily. 'Look, what does it matter if Ellie won't go out with you?' she continued, as he gazed at her unhappily. 'You're always telling me there's plenty more fish in the sea.'

'Not like Ellie, there's not,' he said and then flushed even more as she stared at him in surprise. 'It was you who started it, you know—telling me to ask her out. It got me thinking and the more I thought the more. . .' He came to a halt, seeing her bemused expression. 'Rowan, I'm falling in love with her and she won't give me the time of day.'

She shook her head. 'Oh, Matt, you've really messed up this one.'

'I know, I know,' he said. 'So will you talk to her for me?'

'I'll try.'

'When?' he demanded.

'When the moment's right,' was all she would say and eventually he had to be content with that.

She went back to her work with a wry shake of her head. Of all the girls she would have thought Matt would have fallen in love with, Ellie was the least likely. It had to be a case of opposites attracting. Just like you and Ewan, a little voice whispered, and she crushed down the thought resolutely. Get on with this work, Rowan, she told herself firmly—another half-hour and it will be finished.

She wasn't finished almost an hour later when a sudden noise in the waiting-room outside caught her attention.

For a moment she didn't move and then slowly she got to her feet. Surgeries in London were broken into all the time by people looking for drugs, but she hadn't expected it here.

Quickly she picked up the scissors from her desk—they weren't much of a weapon but they were better than nothing. With a fast-beating heart she edged her way to the door, took a deep breath and then threw it open, only to find herself gazing up into a pair of quizzical blue eyes.

'A simple ''hello'' would be quite sufficient, Rowan!'

A shaky laugh came from her as she lowered the scissors. 'Are you deliberately trying to give me a heart attack, Ewan Moncrieff?' she protested.

'I was walking past and thought Matt must have forgotten to switch off all the lights,' he smiled. 'What are you doing here?'

'Trying to catch up on some paperwork,' she answered, going back to her desk, only to see him deliberately unhook her coat from the back of the door and hold it out to her.

'Home, Rowan.'

'But these files—'

'Leave them,' he ordered. 'They can wait for one day and, as Tilly said, you look exhausted.'

'I only need another half-hour—'

'Home, Rowan,' he repeated.

'Hey, don't get bossy on me!' she chuckled.

'With you, it's the only way,' he declared. 'Come on, I'll walk you home and in return you can invite me up for a cup of coffee.'

She paused in mid-stride to gaze up at him uncertainly. 'Coffee?'

'Liquid drink—can be taken black, or with cream or milk—'

'I know what coffee is,' she interrupted.

'But you're wondering if that's all I'm asking to come up for, aren't you?' he said gently.

She coloured.

'I told you, lass, I'm a patient man,' he said with a soft smile. 'Coffee's what I asked for and coffee is all I expect to get.'

She took a deep breath. 'In that case, why don't we stop at the fish and chip shop—get something to go with that coffee?'

'Now you're talking,' he declared. 'I'm starving.'

'You're always starving!' she laughed as she followed him out of the surgery.

It didn't take long to pick up the fish and chips, though the curious stares and nudges their presence together occasioned left her feeling distinctly rattled.

'Living here's like living in a goldfish bowl,' she said vexedly as she led the way into her flat.

'You'll get used to it,' he replied.

'Perhaps,' she murmured. 'Why don't you sit down?' she added quickly, feeling his gaze upon her. 'You look like a salesman standing there.'

He stared at her for a moment and then a flash of irritation appeared on his face. 'Why is this damned place always so cold?' he demanded.

'The central heating system plays up occasionally. Give the radiator a thump with that book—that usually starts it.'

His eyebrows lifted slightly and then he did as she suggested.

'This flat is a dump,' he observed as a clanking, gurgling sound filled the air.

'Thanks a lot!' she exclaimed. 'I've just spent a small fortune emulsioning the walls and now you tell me I've got rotten taste!'

'You know what I mean,' he declared. 'And the thing is. . .the thing is, I chose this flat for you.'

'I know you did.'

He stared at her in surprise. 'How long have you known?'

'From the first night. I guessed it was your not very subtle way of trying to ensure I didn't stay.'

'It was a lousy thing to do,' he said, shamefaced.

'It damned nearly worked, I can tell you,' she laughed.

'We'll have to find you somewhere else—'

'Will you shut up about the flat and eat these fish and chips before they get cold?' she broke in firmly.

They didn't bother with knives and forks or plates. They simply sat down on the sitting-room floor and ate the fish and chips out of the brown paper wrappings with their fingers.

'You know, if I'm not careful, I'll get as bad as you—living off scratch meals,' she observed, licking her fingers with relish.

'It's an occupational hazard, I'm afraid,' he sighed. 'We're so damn busy telling everyone else what they should and shouldn't eat that we don't have time to prepare proper meals for ourselves, which is probably why so many doctors end up having heart attacks.'

'If you keep on creeping up on me I won't need to bother about my cholesterol levels—I'll just drop dead on the spot!' she chuckled, and as he threw back his head and laughed her heart contracted.

Why was she so attracted to this man? Was it simply because she was lonely—because, after Colin, it was flattering to think that someone found her desirable—or was it more than that?

The only way she would ever find out would be if she let down her guard. It would be a risk, but if she didn't take that risk—if she shut out all human contact for fear of being hurt again—she would never know what might have been.

'I wish you'd come to the ceilidh with me next week,' he said unexpectedly. 'I'm sure you'd enjoy it.'

'You wouldn't enjoy it very much if I ended up having to leave you halfway through the evening,' she pointed out.

'I might not enjoy it but I'd understand,' he smiled.

And he would understand, she thought. He would never sulk if she had to leave a function early; he would never subject her to the long and bitter silences she'd had to endure at Colin's hands if she was late home for a dinner he was holding. Ewan would always understand, as Colin never had.

'Is your leg really bothering you?' he continued.

'It's fine,' she said, rolling up her trouser leg to show him.

'Not a bad job, if I say so myself,' he commented, surveying his handiwork with a professional eye. 'And you've no pain at all—no discomfort?' he added, running his fingers lightly across the scar.

'No,' she murmured, wondering how it was possible for such a casual touch to have such a devastating effect on her heart rate.

'So will you come—to the ceilidh with me?' he asked again, his eyes fixed on her and his hand still lying lightly on her leg.

Right at this moment I don't think there'd be anything I could refuse you, her mind said.

'OK, I'll come,' she managed to reply and saw him smile.

'Lord, is that the time?' he exclaimed, his eye catching sight of the clock. 'I'd better be going.'

She nodded but as she gazed up at him silently, her eyes two enormous grey pools of uncertainty, he tilted her chin towards him and shook his head.

'Oh, lass, when you look at me like that how's a man supposed to want only coffee?'

She smiled tremulously. 'Ewan—'

'I know, I know. One step at a time,' he said and bent his head and kissed her.

It was scarcely a kiss at all, but it was enough. Then such a wealth of longing coursed through her that it was she who deepened the kiss, she who caught hold of the lapels of his jacket to bring him closer. A soft moan came from her as his tongue gently encircled her mouth and then, almost as though both feared that the moment would not last, their kisses took on an almost frantic, desperate urgency.

Never had she felt this way before—as though her whole body was ablaze with longings that only this man could satisfy. She did not care when her blouse somehow disappeared; she did not care when the fine wisp of her bra was gone.

All she knew was that her body ached for him and when he captured one of her nipples with his mouth and teased it slowly, oh, so slowly, into an aching point with his tongue, she dug her fingers deep into his shoulders, her body shuddering with exquisite pleasure.

Nothing seemed to matter any more; nothing seemed important any more. All that mattered was his hardness against her, her own answering, slippery arousal and the overwhelming desire that was spiralling inside her to have more of him—the knowledge that her body would surely die if it could not have more of him—and then suddenly the moment was shattered by the sharp ringing of her doorbell.

'Ignore it,' she whispered with frustration into his neck.

'We can't,' he said raggedly, reaching for her blouse and slipping it round her shoulders. 'It could be important.'

Never had she thought that she would curse her profession but, as she buttoned her blouse with trembling fingers and went across to the door, she knew that she cursed it now.

Perhaps it was someone who had come to the wrong house; perhaps it was someone looking for directions. Whoever it was had a lousy sense of timing, she decided as she threw open the door, only to stare in stunned disbelief at the figure on the doorstep.

'*Colin!*'

'In the flesh,' he grinned.

She gazed at him in confusion. A few months ago this would have been the happiest moment of her life and yet now—

'Aren't you going to ask me in?' he continued.

'Yes...yes, of course.' She stood aside quickly, desperately trying to collect her thoughts.

'I'm sorry, I didn't realise you had company,' he said as his eyes fell on Ewan.

She took a deep breath. 'Colin, this is Ewan Moncrieff. Ewan, this is...this is Colin Renton.'

The two men nodded to one another but they did not, she noticed, shake hands.

'You should have told me you were coming, Colin,' she murmured. 'This isn't a good time—'

'I didn't know I was coming myself until this morning. Look, can we talk—alone I mean?' he added pointedly.

She glanced uncertainly from him to Ewan and then back again.

'It's OK, Rowan,' Ewan said quietly. 'I know when I'm not wanted.'

'It isn't that,' she faltered. 'It's just that as Colin's come all this way—'

'I understand,' he said, beginning to walk towards the door.

No, no, you don't, her heart cried. How can you possibly understand when even I don't know how I feel?

'Ewan, wait!'

He turned towards her and she gazed at him silently. What could she say, what could she possibly say with Colin standing there—with her own emotions so tangled that she didn't know what she wanted any more?

'I'll. . .I'll see you tomorrow,' she said, her eyes begging for understanding.

He gazed at her for a long moment and then nodded and was gone.

'Strange bloke,' Colin observed as she turned towards him, her face troubled.

'Why did you come, Colin. . .? Why, after all this time, did you come?' she demanded.

'Because I realised that walking out on you was the biggest mistake I'd ever made in my life,' he said gently. 'I had to come to say I was sorry and to ask you to come back.'

Did he really think that just saying he was sorry was enough? she wondered. Did he really think that it would erase all those nights she'd cried herself to sleep, all those days when the ache inside her was so acute that it was like a physical pain? And then as she gazed at him he suddenly smiled, and it was the smile she knew so well—the smile that used to make her forgive him anything.

Abruptly she turned from him.

'Can we talk about this tomorrow, Colin? I've had a long day and I'm tired. Go back to your hotel and I promise we'll talk tomorrow.'

'I was hoping I could stay with you,' he replied uncomfortably.

'With me?' she echoed.

'I didn't realise this was the start of the salmon-fishing season and there's not a bed to be had anywhere. The couch or the floor would be fine,' he added quickly as a frown appeared on her forehead. 'I know I just can't walk back into your life as though nothing had happened.'

Too true you can't, she thought, but she'd shared two years of her life with this man, two years she couldn't just forget in an instant.

'All right, you can stay,' she said, 'but you'll sleep on the couch, Colin.'

He nodded and quickly she went through to the hall and began pulling sheets and blankets from the airing cupboard.

She told herself that she was pleased Colin had arrived when he did. She told herself that his arrival had probably prevented her from making a terrible mistake. But as one of the sheets fell from her arms and she bent to retrieve it she wondered why, if she was so damned grateful, she had never felt more wretched in all her life.

CHAPTER SEVEN

'Now, I'm not one to gossip,' Mrs Ross declared with a look that dared anyone in Canna's small supermarket to suggest otherwise, 'but it's not right—it's simply not right.'

'What's not right, Mrs Ross?' Mary Finlay asked with a sigh of resignation.

'Dr Rowan living with that young man.'

'We don't actually know that he *is* living with her,' Doris Jones observed as she stared into the deep-freeze cabinet, trying to make up her mind between the fish and the chicken. 'I heard he was just here on holiday.'

'Well, you can believe that, if you like,' Mrs Ross replied, her ample bosom swelling visibly, 'but I just happened to ask Jamie McNeil how many bedrooms Dr Rowan's flat has, and do you know what he told me?' She paused and then leant forward conspiratorially. '*One*— that's how many bedrooms that flat has, and you're not telling me a good-looking fellow like Colin Renton is sleeping on the floor.'

'Mrs Ross—'

'I know Dr Rowan comes from London and the morals down there aren't. . .well. . .they aren't what they should be, but you'd think Dr Ewan would have a quiet word with her.'

'Mrs Ross—'

'I mean, these sorts of goings on might be all right in a city, but in Canna we have certain standards.'

'*Mrs Ross!*'

'Will you stop waving your arms at me like some sort of demented windmill, Mary Finlay!' Mrs Ross exclaimed in exasperation. 'I don't see—'

116

No one ever did find out what Mrs Ross didn't see because she had finally noticed what Mary Finlay had been so desperately trying to tell her—that Ewan Moncrieff had emerged from behind a high stack of soup tins, his face taut and white.

Heads were averted uncomfortably and not a word was spoken as he grimly paid for his purchases and left, tight-lipped.

'Well, I don't care if he *did* hear me,' Mrs Ross declared defensively as every eye in the shop turned back to her. 'I stand by what I said—it's not right, it's just not right!'

Ewan didn't think it was right either as he strode down the road, his face like thunder, but then neither did he think it was right that he had a dreadful suspicion that if Colin Renton had suddenly appeared around the corner he would have been sorely tempted to rearrange his handsome features.

You have no claim on her, he told himself as he pushed past Ellie in the waiting-room, cutting off her cheery greeting in mid-flow. She can choose whatever man she wants, he reminded himself as he slammed his consulting-room door shut and threw himself down in his seat.

But as a heart-shaped face with a pair of laughing grey eyes swam in front of him, he groaned out loud and sent his waste-paper bin skidding across the floor with a well-aimed kick.

'Something wrong?' Rowan asked as Ellie appeared in her room, looking distinctly harassed.

'Ewan.'

Rowan sighed. 'He's in a foul mood again?'

'Even worse than yesterday, if that's possible. What's the matter with him, Rowan?'

'Forget about Ewan for the moment,' she replied, deliberately changing the subject. 'There's something I want to talk to you about and now's as good a time as any. It's Matt.'

The receptionist's face set. 'What about Matt?'

'He's asked me to try and persuade you to go out with him.'

'Has he, indeed?' Ellie snapped, her brown eyes sparkling. 'Well, he's got some nerve, I'll say that for him!'

'But you like him—you told me so,' Rowan said gently. 'Look, I know he flirts a little—OK, so he flirts a lot,' she added as the girl's eyebrows rose, 'but I really think he's serious this time. Will you go out with him—even if it's just the once?'

Ellie said nothing for a moment and then a small smile appeared on her face. 'OK, tell him I'll do it on one condition.'

'What's that?'

'No one knows.'

'But you can't keep something like that a secret around here—it's impossible,' Rowan exclaimed.

'If he's really as keen as you say he is he'll find a way,' Ellie declared. 'I'm not going to be known as one of Matt's cast-offs, Rowan.'

'But, Ellie—'

Rowan came to a halt as her door swung open.

'Is there any possibility we might get morning surgery started some time today, Ellie?' Ewan demanded. 'It's five past nine and I haven't seen a patient yet!'

Ellie gulped and nodded. 'See what I mean?' she said expressively as he strode away.

'Another fun-packed morning,' Rowan sighed. 'OK, Ellie. Send in my first patient.'

It was a long morning but as she listened sympathetically to Mrs Murray's worries about her mother's angina, gave Bill Terry his yellow fever injection for his forthcoming holiday to Africa, and explained Mrs Arnold's blood test results, she made up her mind. It was one thing for Ewan to take out his anger and hurt on her but to do it to Ellie and Matt was unforgivable and she was going to put a stop to it.

'Last patient coming up, Rowan,' Ellie declared as her consulting-room clock showed eleven o'clock. 'It's Mairi Fisher—and she's on her own.'

That in itself was a surprise but so also was the look of nervous determination on the girl's face as she sat down. She took a deep breath, opened her mouth and then, to Rowan's dismay, promptly burst into tears.

'Mrs Fisher—Mairi—what's the matter, what's wrong?' Rowan exclaimed, reaching across the desk to grasp Mairi's hands in hers.

'Oh, Doctor, I'm so ashamed,' she sobbed. 'I'm only twenty-five...I thought it only happened to old people or to children...I'm so ashamed...so ashamed...'

'Now, listen to me, Mairi,' Rowan said as the girl's tears started to flow again, 'there is nothing you can say to me that I probably haven't heard a hundred times before, so tell me what's troubling you.'

And bit by bit the story came out. That since Beth's birth Mairi had been experiencing incontinence problems, problems she'd hoped would go away but they hadn't—they'd simply got worse and worse.

It was so obvious now, Rowan thought as she held the girl's hands tightly. Mairi's many visits to the surgery, when she must have been trying to pluck up the courage to say what was wrong, her over-liberal use of perfume because she was terrified that someone might smell the urine from her.

'Oh, Mairi, why ever didn't you tell us before?' she said gently. 'It's a very common problem. All that's wrong is that your pelvic floor muscles must have become weak. It could be due to childbirth or even something as simple as a chronic cough or constipation. I can give you a leaflet outlining some exercises—'

'I've done exercises—for months and months after

Beth was born I did exercises—but it hasn't made any difference,' Mairi hiccuped.

'Then the first thing we need to do is arrange for you to see a gynaecologist. There's nothing to worry about,' she added as the girl gazed at her in alarm. 'The gynaecologist will simply do some tests on your bladder to find out why there's a leakage.'

'And then?' Mairi whispered.

'Once we know what the situation is we'll probably start you off with a course of drugs and then arrange some sessions with the physiotherapist. She'll check to see if you're doing the exercises properly. Or we could try electrical treatment—that's where we stimulate the muscles artificially to make them stronger.'

'But what if all of that doesn't work?'

'Then there's a whole host of other things we can try—even an operation, which has very good results.'

'So I can be cured?' Mairi said tremulously.

'There's every likelihood you can be.'

'Oh, Doctor, I thought I was going to be like this for the rest of my life and I was so ashamed—'

'There's no need to be,' Rowan broke in firmly. 'You wouldn't believe how many women suffer in silence with a similar problem.'

'Truly?'

'Truly,' Rowan smiled. 'Now, I'll write to the gynaecologist today and we can start to get this sorted out. Oh, and, Mairi,' she added, as the girl stood up to go, 'you don't need the perfume—no one can smell you, honestly.'

So she'd been right and Ewan had been wrong, Rowan thought as Mairi went out of the door, looking as though a huge weight had been taken off her shoulders. Mairi hadn't just been an over-protective mother but a very worried young woman, who had just been too embarrassed to reveal what was really wrong with her. And yet she told me, Rowan thought with pleasure. She trusted me enough to tell me. It was a good feeling, a very good feeling indeed.

'Sorry, Rowan,' Ellie said as she stuck her head round the consulting-room door, 'but Ewan would like to know if you're going to be much longer—he wants to start the practice meeting.'

'In other words, he said, "Get along that damn corridor, Ellie, and tell Rowan I don't have all bloody day"!'

The receptionist giggled. 'Pretty accurate, I'm afraid. What shall I tell him?'

'Five minutes—tell him I'll be there in five minutes.'

It was one of the shortest practice meetings she'd ever sat in on and also one of the most uncomfortable. Ewan said hardly a word but his brooding presence was all too pervasive, and neither she nor Matt were completely successful in disguising their relief when he finally declared the meeting closed.

'That was fun,' Matt muttered in an undertone as he collected the dirty coffee-cups. 'Any idea what's up with him?'

She shook her head, refusing to be drawn.

'I've had a word with Ellie,' she whispered. 'She'll go out with you as long as no one knows.'

'But's that's impossible—'

'Are you going to the ceilidh tonight?' she said brightly, noticing Ewan's gaze upon them, curious and irritated.

'Wouldn't miss it—how about you?'

She nodded. 'I thought I'd take Colin. He's hardly been anywhere since he got here, what with me working—'

'You can hardly expect to get holiday leave when you've only been here four months,' Ewan snapped.

'I don't recall asking for any,' she said smoothly, though her colour deepened.

Matt edged towards the door. 'I think—if no one minds—I think I might just get on with the morning rounds,' he declared, and promptly made his escape.

Ewan reached for his folders, clearly intending to go too, and Rowan gritted her teeth.

'We need to talk.'

'I don't have time, Rowan—'

'Then make time,' she said. 'Look, I'm sorry about the ceilidh tonight—I know I said I'd go with you—'

'You don't have to explain—I understand,' he interrupted tightly, making for the door.

'Ewan, talk to me—'

He paused, his face taut. 'What's there to talk about? That night. . .you were lonely and unhappy and I just happened to be there. I understand.'

She cut across him quickly and closed the staff-room door with a bang.

'Do you realise how deeply insulting you're being?' she said, her voice unsteady and her grey eyes dark. 'Yes, I was lonely; yes, I was unhappy, but you make it sound as though you could have been the. . .the postman or the milkman, for all the difference it would have made to me.'

'I think you like me—'

'*Like* you?' she exclaimed. 'Do you think I would have. . .have behaved as I did if all I felt for you was just a *liking*?'

'But Colin—'

'What about Colin?'

He glanced away from her and dawning comprehension came into her eyes.

'You think I'm sleeping with him, don't you?' she said. 'That's what this is all about, isn't it?'

His face tightened. 'Your private life is your own.'

'Too true it is, but I thought you would have credited me with a little pride, if nothing else,' she replied with difficulty. 'Colin walked out on me, Ewan. I hadn't heard from him in almost a year. Do you honestly believe that I'd jump straight into bed with him after that?'

'I know you loved him—'

'I don't forget or forgive that easily, Ewan.'

'So you're not—?'

'Colin sleeps on the couch. He doesn't like it but he does.'

He took an uneven breath. 'He wants you back, doesn't he?'

She nodded.

'And are you. . .going back to him?'

She gazed up at him, into his deep blue eyes. 'I have to at least give him a chance to explain, Ewan. Maybe a lot of the fault was mine. . .devoting so much of my time to my work. . .I don't know. I only know that I loved him once and I can't just pretend those two years didn't happen.'

He put out a hand towards her and then let it fall.

'What are you doing for the rest of the morning?'

'Colin and I are going shopping and then I thought we might grab a quick lunch before my clinic this afternoon.'

'Let me take you both out to lunch—by way of a peace offering for my behaviour this week.'

'Lunch?' she repeated and then gazed at him warily. 'Where exactly did you have in mind?'

'The Swan,' he answered. 'Why—where did you think I had in mind?'

Laughter was plain in his eyes and she chuckled.

'You can't blame a girl for being careful, can you?' she said.

He grinned. 'We've had some good times, haven't we?'

He made it sound as though he'd already accepted that she would go back to Colin, but going back to Colin meant that she would never again see the man who stood so awkwardly in front of her, would never see that swift smile that so illuminated his dark face or those deep blue eyes which were so disturbing. It was an overwhelmingly depressing thought.

'Ewan—'

'So, will you let me take you both out to lunch?' he said as he led the way along the corridor to the surgery door.

She smiled. 'I'd like that—I'd like that very much.'

Colin wasn't nearly so enthusiastic when she told him of Ewan's invitation after they'd finished their shopping.

'Do we have to?' he protested. 'We haven't been able to go into one single shop this morning without someone collaring you for a consultation, and the last thing I need is a medical lunch as well!'

'We won't talk shop, I promise,' she insisted.

'You've no private life at all—you realise that, don't you?' he declared as they crossed the road to the Swan just as the village clock struck one. 'You're a doctor twenty-four hours a day.'

'It's not that bad—'

'Rowan, we couldn't even go to the bank without that woman thanking you for the pills you'd prescribed for her eczema and that girl asking you to do a quick examination of her new baby!'

She chuckled. 'I have to admit it used to drive me mad but I rather like it now—it makes me feel accepted, part of the community.'

He shook his head. 'It's called abusing your good nature. You're entitled to time off like everyone else.'

She didn't say anything. It wasn't worth the argument and she sensed argument there would be if she tried to defend her work.

Ewan was waiting for them at the hotel and, to her relief, by the time they'd got a table Colin had thrown off his irritation and was a pleasant and witty companion throughout the whole meal.

She left him to do most of the talking, mindful of his gibe about talking shop but also because it gave her the opportunity to gaze across at the two men with ease.

Colin was so handsome with his blond hair, deep brown eyes and immaculate city suit, whereas Ewan—

She chuckled inwardly. The Queen could have been coming to lunch and she doubted whether he would have thought to put on something other than his Harris tweed jacket and corduroys.

He wasn't handsome, not in the way Colin was handsome. His features were too harsh without the softening influence of laughter, but as he caught her gaze upon him his lips curved into a smile so tender that a warm glow spread through her, a glow that seemed to reach down into her very being, and she found herself smiling back, oblivious of Colin's deep frown.

She kept her promise about not talking shop until they were enjoying their coffee, and then she couldn't resist telling Ewan about Mairi Fisher.

'So you were right and I was wrong,' he declared. 'Well done.'

'It makes a change, doesn't it?' she laughed, only to sigh as she heard the clock on the mantelpiece in the dining-room chime two. 'I have to go, I'm afraid. If I don't hurry I'll be late for my clinic—though I doubt if the few women who have turned up will mind waiting a few minutes.'

'Still having problems persuading the women to come forward?' Ewan said as they all got to their feet.

'It's getting better,' she conceded, 'but there's still an awful lot of resistance. Sorry, Colin,' she added, seeing his bored expression, 'I promised I wouldn't talk shop and I'm doing just that.'

He shrugged. 'I'm used to it. Just don't be late this evening, Rowan,' he continued as they made their way outside. 'We're going to the ceilidh, remember, and you know how I hate arriving late anywhere.'

'I won't be late, I promise,' she said as she waved him goodbye.

'That was a mistake,' Ewan observed as he gazed thoughtfully along the road.

'What was a mistake?' she asked.

'Promising what you just did—look down there.'

She turned in the direction of his gaze and gasped out loud. There wasn't a vacant space in the car park outside the surgery.

'What on earth's happened?' she exclaimed, quickening her stride.

'Either your clinic's taken off in a big way or we've got an outbreak of measles,' Ewan grinned.

'Funny man,' she replied dourly, swinging into the surgery, only to stop dead in her tracks.

The place was packed with women of all ages—some sitting on seats, some perched on the window-ledges, others standing in clusters round the walls—and in the middle of it all stood a very harassed Ellie.

'If you think this is busy you should have been here half an hour ago,' the receptionist declared, clearly torn between delight and consternation. 'I don't know how we're going to manage. They all want cervical smears, Rowan, and your clinic only lasts three hours.'

'Can I help?' Ewan asked. 'I could give you an hour or so if that would lighten your load a bit.'

A large, instantly recognisable figure with flaming red hair thrust her way purposefully through the throng.

'I'm sorry, Dr Ewan,' Annie Galbraith declared firmly, 'but it's the lady doctor we've all come to see—no offence meant to you, of course.'

'None taken, Annie,' Ewan said with some amusement. 'Sorry, Rowan,' he added, turning to her apologetically, 'but it would appear you're on your own.'

And with that he was gone.

'It's all Annie Galbraith's doing,' Ellie announced as she followed Rowan through to her consulting-room. 'She's been round all her friends and bullied them into coming.'

'But how?' Rowan demanded. 'What did she say to them?'

'I don't know—she wouldn't tell me. Shall I send her in first?'

Rowan nodded. Whatever Annie had said to her friends it had certainly worked and she couldn't wait to find out what it was.

'Now I'll have you know, Doctor, that I don't usually hold with people poking about my private areas looking for trouble,' Annie Galbraith declared as she settled her ample form on one of the seats, 'but you went up that mountain to help my Robbie so I've decided the least I can do is have this smear thing done.'

'I'm very pleased to hear it, Annie,' Rowan replied, 'but all these other women—?'

'They wouldn't come before because they were feared of finding out the worst but, as I said to them, if you could conquer your fear to help one of my lads then we could conquer our fear, too.'

Rowan stared at Annie in wonder. She'd lost count of the number of posters she'd put up in shops, asking women to come forward to be tested. She'd talked herself hoarse at WRI meetings on the benefits of regular screening procedures, and none of her efforts had worked.

This one woman had single-handedly persuaded half the women in the area to come to the surgery because she'd conquered her fear of heights. It was humbling in the extreme.

'Thank you, Annie,' she said huskily. 'Oh, *thank you*!'

The rest of the afternoon sped by in an exhausting round of examinations, and she couldn't believe it when she looked at her clock and discovered that it was seven o'clock.

'Thanks for staying so late, Ellie,' she said as the girl came in to collect the samples she'd taken.

'I wouldn't have missed it for the world,' Ellie beamed. 'It was a bit like the January sales, wasn't it?'

'Something like that,' Rowan chuckled. 'You'd better get off home—you must be exhausted.'

'Not so exhausted I can't dance the night away.'

Rowan gazed at her in confusion and then groaned. The ceilidh—she'd completely forgotten about the ceilidh!

Despite them both working flat out to pack up the samples, it was almost eight o'clock before she got back to her flat and one look at Colin's face told her that he was furious.

'Look, I really am sorry,' she began contritely, 'but my clinic—'

'You know as well as I do that if it hadn't been your bloody clinic it would have been something else,' he snapped. 'Some emergency you couldn't ignore—some forms you just had to fill in!'

'We can still go,' she protested. 'Just give me three-quarters of an hour to wash and change—'

'Was it too much to expect you to keep your promise?' he interrupted angrily. 'God knows, I haven't asked for much since I've been here but I thought you could have kept one lousy promise!'

'I didn't mean to be late—honestly I didn't—but Annie Galbraith—'

'Spare me the details,' he retorted. 'Just get changed!'

She was so tired. All she really wanted was a long hot bath and no emergency calls but she had promised, and a promise was a promise. Quickly she washed her hair and showered and then rifled through her wardrobe for something suitable to wear. It couldn't be anything fancy in case she was called away, and eventually she opted for a plain green woollen dress with a deep white lace collar and cuffs.

'Is that it?' Colin said bluntly when he saw her. 'Is that what you're wearing?'

'I'm on call, remember—'

'But I thought you were going to try and get your rota changed,' he exclaimed. 'You didn't even ask, did you?' he added as she flushed. 'You didn't even bloody ask—well, thanks, Rowan—thanks for nothing!'

She bit her lip. 'Please don't do this, Colin. It's been a long day and I don't want to fight with you.'

He shook his head. 'I'm sorry, but it's this damned job of yours—it's always been this damned job.'

'Colin—'

'We could be good together, you know we could. My boss likes you—he's always saying how bright you are, what a perfect corporate wife you'd make and how stupid I was to let you go. I want to marry you, Rowan. I want you to give up this foolishness and come back to London and marry me.'

She stiffened. 'This foolishness?'

'Giving so much of yourself to your patients and so little to me. Your job's always been the wedge between us. If you weren't a doctor we wouldn't fight—I know we wouldn't.'

She stared back at him. He didn't love her and she knew now with startling clarity that she didn't love him. She'd been dazzled by his good looks, had been flattered when all her friends had said how lucky she was.

For two years she'd tried to fit into his world, to be what he wanted her to be, and when he'd walked out she'd blamed herself. But she wasn't to blame. It just would never have worked.

'I can't marry you, Colin.'

'Look, this probably wasn't the best time to ask—'

A wry smile appeared on her lips. 'Actually, it was the very best time and I meant what I said—I can't marry you.'

'But I love you—'

'No, you don't,' she said gently. 'If you did, you wouldn't ask me to give up my work.'

'It's just a *job*, Rowan!' he exclaimed.

She shook her head. 'My medicine is as much a part of me as the colour of my hair or my eyes, Colin. I could never give it up.'

His jaw set. 'It's me or the job, Rowan—you can't have both.'

'I think loving someone—truly loving someone—means loving them without conditions, Colin,' she said with a sad smile.

'And you think that refugee from a charity shop can give you that?' he demanded.

She coloured. 'If you're meaning Ewan, we're friends, colleagues—'

'Of course you are,' he broke in caustically. 'It could only be a meeting of minds for you, couldn't it, Rowan—you don't function from the waist down, do you?'

She flushed scarlet. 'Colin—'

'You don't have to say any more,' he interrupted. 'You've made your position quite clear so let's get on to this ceilidh thing before it's finished.'

'You still want to go?' she said in surprise.

'What else do you suggest we do for the rest of the evening?' he said grimly. 'Sit in this God-awful flat, staring at one another all night?'

The ceilidh was already in full swing by the time they arrived, and one glance at the women's dresses and the men's kilts told Rowan that Colin had been right—she was completely under-dressed for the occasion but it couldn't be helped. For a moment she stood indecisively on the threshold and then saw Ellie and Matt waving to them.

'We've been saving these seats for the pair of you,' Matt declared when they had pushed their way through to him. 'And it wasn't an easy task, I can assure you— by the end of the evening people will kill for a seat!'

She chuckled as she sat down. 'You look lovely, Ellie.'

And she did. Her soft rose dress set off her dark features to perfection.

'What's up with Colin?' Matt frowned as he strode

off in the direction of the bar without a word.

'Don't ask,' she sighed.

'Oh, look, there's Ewan,' Ellie exclaimed. 'Ewan—Ewan, over here!' she called, beckoning to him.

Rowan stared in stunned amazement as he came towards them in full Highland dress. Only this afternoon she had decided that this man wasn't handsome. Oh, boy, do you need your eyes tested, Rowan, she decided. In full Highland dress and with a broad smile illuminating his face, this man was handsome—devastatingly handsome.

'You make me feel like Cinderella,' she laughed up at him shakily.

'I don't see why,' he said softly. 'I think you look beautiful—but, then, I'd think you'd look beautiful in a bin liner.'

'You say the nicest things, Ewan Moncrieff,' she chuckled.

'Gospel truth at all times, Rowan,' he grinned. 'Come on, let's dance.'

She hadn't enjoyed herself at a function so much for ages. All the dances were Scottish country ones, which meant that energy and staying power were more important than skill, but she couldn't help noticing as the evening wore on that though she might be enjoying herself Colin was not.

'You can't force him to have fun, Rowan,' Matt observed, seeing her frown as he whirled her round his arm during an energetic Gay Gordons.

'But all he's done is prop up the bar all night, Matt,' she protested.

'Well, if it makes him happy—?'

'Unfortunately, I don't think it has,' she replied.

'Ewan's going over to him,' Matt observed. 'Maybe he'll cheer him up.'

Colin didn't want to be cheered up and he certainly didn't want Ewan Moncrieff's company.

'Come to gloat, have you, Ewan?' he said thickly, raising his glass to him and slopping most of the contents onto the floor in the process.

'Look, why don't I drive you back to Rowan's flat?' Ewan suggested as Colin swayed precariously towards him. 'It wouldn't take ten minutes—'

'She's given me the brush-off, you know,' Colin continued, shaking off Ewan's steadying hand with irritation, 'so if you're interested in the frigid bitch, be my guest.'

Ewan's eyebrows lowered ominously. 'Keep your voice down, Colin.'

'Don't like the truth, eh?' he smiled. 'Well, it is the truth. The only thing that's ever got that girl excited is her bloody job.'

'I think you've said enough—'

'She's lousy in bed, you know,' Colin broke in with a loud hiccup.

'If you don't shut your mouth right now I swear to God I'll shut it for you,' Ewan said, his voice ice-cold.

'Why?' Colin demanded with an ugly laugh. 'Don't you think she'd like her precious patients to know that as a doctor she may be Miss Wonderful but as a woman she's got about as much sex drive as a fish? Listen, people of Canna,' he continued, swaying round on his feet to face the crowded dance floor, 'Dr Rowan—'

He didn't get a chance to say any more. Ewan's fist collided with his nose, sending him crashing back against one of the tables. There was the sound of breaking glass, the band came to a discordant halt, someone screamed and then half the room rushed over, Matt and Rowan amongst them.

'What happened?' she demanded in confusion, glancing from Colin's bloody face to Ewan's grazed knuckles.

Neither man said a word and, all too conscious of the

audience gathered round them, Rowan helped Colin to his feet, her cheeks red.

'I think the floor appears to have proved rather too slippery for my friend,' she laughed shakily. 'Ewan, can you help me get him home?' she added, with a look that brooked no opposition.

The crowd parted silently in front of them, but the walk to the door was the longest of Rowan's life. She doubted if there was a person there who believed a word she'd said but at least no one had contradicted her to her face—they'd do plenty of that when they'd gone.

'OK, what happened?' she demanded as soon as they were safely outside.

Colin wiped the blood from his nose with an unsteady hand. 'I said something Ewan disagreed with.'

'Is this true?' she asked, turning to Ewan.

Almost imperceptibly he nodded.

'Colin said something you disagreed with so you *hit* him?' she gasped. 'What could he have said—what could *anyone* have said that would have provoked such a reaction?'

Deliberately Ewan avoided her gaze and she exploded.

'I don't understand you. . .I thought I knew you but I obviously don't! Ewan, please, just give me one good reason—just one—to explain why you would cause a scene that's going to be the talk of Canna for the rest of time!'

'How about I was trying for a new image?' he suggested with an attempt at a smile that deceived neither of them. 'Goodbye, dull Ewan, hello, Mr Action Man?'

'If you're going to make a joke out of it then I've got nothing else to say to you,' she said tightly, turning on her heel.

'Rowan, it wasn't what you think!' he called after her as she took Colin's arm to guide his unsteady steps, but she didn't turn round and just kept on walking towards her car.

The drunk on her arm was the man she had once thought she loved, and the man who had just hit him was the man she knew she was falling in love with. Oh, Rowan, she thought bleakly, have you got lousy taste in men.

CHAPTER EIGHT

'Two full cartons of naproxen, two half-boxes of diazepam—'

'When are you going to give Ewan a break, Rowan? It's been three weeks now since the ceilidh—'

'Four half-boxes of temazepam, six—no, sorry Ellie—make that seven full boxes of small steri-strips—'

'Colin's gone back to London and people are beginning to forget—'

Rowan turned quickly in the store cupboard, her grey eyes flashing and her colour high.

'*Forget!*' she exclaimed. 'No one's ever going to forget, Ellie, and the damnable thing is that they all blame me. Oh, yes, they do,' she continued as the girl tried to interrupt. 'I didn't hit Colin, I wasn't the one who caused the scene, but I know damn fine what they're all saying—"We never had these sorts of goings-on until *she* arrived" and "None of our doctors ever behaved like this until *she* joined the practice!"'

'But, Rowan—'

'I'd just begun to live down that disaster with Alec Mackenzie and then Ewan has to go and do this—oh, I could *kill* him, Ellie!'

The receptionist's lips twitched. 'Don't you think that might make matters worse?'

Rowan's face set belligerently. 'Probably, but it would make me feel a whole lot better, I can tell you!'

Ellie sighed as she gathered the inventory forms they'd been filling in. 'I take it he's still not saying why he did it?'

Rowan shook her head. 'He just purses his lips like so, frowns like this and clams up totally.'

'Which is why you're giving him the cold shoulder treatment?'

'Exactly,' Rowan declared as she locked the drugs cupboard door behind them, only to lapse into silence as Ewan came down the corridor towards them.

'Is that you finished already?' he said in surprise.

'With Rowan helping, it was a breeze this time,' Ellie smiled and then glanced awkwardly from Rowan's closed face to Ewan's uncomfortable one. 'Well, I guess—if nobody wants me—I'd better get back to the office.'

Silence was her only reply and, with a defeated shrug, she went.

'Miserable day,' Ewan observed, staring at the rain-soaked window.

'Yes.'

'Looks like we might have to forget about April showers this year and settle for storm-force winds and torrential rain instead.'

'Yes.'

'Rowan—'

'Mrs Lennox's blood test results are back. She does have anaemia, as you thought, but Fred Carter's got the all-clear so we'll have to do a re-think about him.'

'Rowan, please—'

'When you've time, could you take a look at Ian Darnley's notes for me? He could just be suffering from panic attacks, but I've a feeling there's a whole lot more to it than that.'

'Rowan, this is crazy!' he exclaimed, raking his hand through his black hair in exasperation. 'How many times do I have to say I'm sorry?'

'You can say you're sorry until the cows come home, as far as I'm concerned,' she replied evenly. 'Until you tell me why you hit Colin—and I want a believable reason, Ewan, not some of the cock-and-bull tales you've come up with—the only conversation you'll get from me will be about our patients.'

'Does it matter?' he protested. 'In the greater scheme of things, does it really matter?'

She met his gaze. 'Yes, it matters. It matters because Colin went to that ceilidh at my invitation; it matters because I've got landed with the blame over something I'd no part in, and it matters because I don't like secrets.'

'I don't make a habit of hitting people, if that's what you're worried about,' he declared with a smile.

'Just Colin?'

His smile vanished. 'He's part of your past—can't you just forget about him, about that night?'

She shook her head. 'He won't ever be truly a part of my past until you tell me what happened.'

His eyes caught and held hers. 'I'm sorry but I can't do that.'

'Then, I'm sorry too,' she said, turning on her heel and striding quickly along the corridor.

Was she just being foolish? she wondered. Was she just making more of this than she should? She shook her head. She had thought she'd known Colin and it had turned out that she hadn't known him at all, and she wasn't about to make the same mistake again with Ewan.

'I thought this was your day off?' Matt said as he came out of his room and almost collided with her.

'I've been helping Ellie with the drugs cupboard inventory,' she said with an effort.

'You spend too much time here,' he frowned. 'You should get out more—socialise.'

'I'm happy as I am,' she said lightly and then, after a quick glance over her shoulder, pushed him deliberately back into his room, her grey eyes sparkling.

'You've got to put me out of my misery, Matt,' she begged. 'You and Ellie—how are things going?'

'You're getting as bad as everyone else round here—nosy as hell,' he protested.

She pouted. 'Ellie won't tell me anything either and I

don't want any details—honestly—all I want to know is if things are going OK.'

He grinned. 'Things are better than OK—things are great.'

'Well, I've got to hand it to you,' she observed. 'I haven't heard so much as a whisper about the two of you—how are you managing it?'

'Elementary, my dear Watson,' he said darkly and then laughed. 'We drive out of Canna in opposite directions and then we cut back to a pre-arranged spot, where Ellie gets out of her car and into mine and then we drive to a restaurant or a pub as far away from Canna as we can.'

A peal of laughter came from Rowan. 'My God, you make it sound as though you've joined MI5!'

'It feels like it too at times!' he said, his eyes dancing. 'But it's working and that's the main thing. I could give you and Ewan a list of pubs and restaurants—'

'Forget it, Matt,' she said quickly.

'He's in love with you, Rowan.'

'Maybe he is and maybe he isn't, but it's really none of your business, is it?' she replied.

'Fair enough,' he said with a shrug, 'but if you'd like someone to knock some sense into him I did some amateur boxing at university.'

'Are you trying to make me completely beyond the pale around here?' she protested. 'My reputation's bad enough, without you and Ewan brawling out in the street!'

His eyes gleamed. 'Boy, but what I wouldn't give to see Mrs Ross's face if we did!'

'Well, keep it in your imagination, please,' she chuckled, and then sighed. 'Oh, Matt, you've no idea how sometimes I long for the anonymity of a city—to be able to go where I want and do what I want without being eternally scrutinised all the time.'

The laughter disappeared from his face.

'Look, don't let the nosy old biddies like Mrs Ross

get under your skin. Think about the women who come
to your clinic, women like Annie Galbraith and Ishbel
Coghill. Do you think they give a damn about your
private life?'

'I guess not,' she said uncertainly, 'but, oh, Matt, there
are times—!'

'Aren't there just?' he grinned. 'Look, if the gossiping
really bothers you that much why don't you give them
something to really talk about?'

'Such as?'

'You and Ewan.'

'Goodbye, Matt,' she said firmly as she reached for
her coat and bag.

He meant well, she knew he did, but she also knew
that if she was going to put her heart on the line again,
if she was going to risk being hurt again, she had to be
certain and she wasn't certain—she wasn't certain about
anything any more.

'Hey, what's up?' she asked as she passed the office
door and saw a deep frown on Ellie's face.

'Oh, it just drives me mad, that's all,' the girl
exclaimed with irritation. 'Every morning it's the same—
people waiting until the last moment to call the office
when they want a home visit.'

'Ewan's left already, I take it?'

'More than half an hour ago. If Mrs Dean had only
phoned about her son earlier he could have called in
there first, instead of having to backtrack.'

'This Mrs Dean—her son's name wouldn't be Billy,
would it?'

'You know him?'

Rowan nodded. 'I met him once in Riochan after he'd
fallen off a roof. Did his mother say what was wrong
with him?'

'Flu, she reckons—not surprising really as half the
neighbourhood's got it.'

'I'll go.'

'But I thought you were going shopping?' Ellie protested.

'It can wait,' Rowan smiled.

'Glutton for punishment!' Ellie called after her as she opened the surgery door and made a run for her car, her head bent low against the driving wind and rain.

She wasn't a glutton for punishment, she thought as she drove out of Canna, her windscreen wipers working overtime in an attempt to combat the torrential rain—she was doing this simply to occupy her mind.

When she worked she didn't think and when she was treating patients she didn't remember, but without those diversions the memories came flooding back—the memories of that night when Colin had arrived and what would surely have happened if he hadn't come.

Even now, she could hardly believe the depths of passion Ewan had aroused in her. Even now, when she shut her eyes and remembered how she'd behaved hot colour would come flooding over her cheeks.

Why, oh, why, she wondered, did she seem to have the unerring ability to fall in love with the wrong man? Because when it comes to men, Rowan Sinclair, you truly are a glutton for punishment, came back the answer, and a bitter smile crossed her face as she drove up the track leading to Mrs Dean's cottage.

She scarcely had time to bring her car to a halt before Fiona Dean was there, her face chalk-white with worry.

'Oh, Doctor, I'm so pleased you've come!' she cried. 'I'm that worried about Billy. He's so pale and—'

'Show me where he is,' Rowan interrupted, pulling her bag from the car.

'I'm probably just overreacting,' Fiona declared, twisting her hands convulsively as she led the way into the house and through to a small bedroom. 'He'll have the flu—that will be all it is—'

'Could you open the curtains for me, Mrs Dean?'

Rowan said as she took her stethoscope from her bag. 'It's a bit dark in here.'

'I had to keep them closed,' Fiona apologised as she reached for them. 'Billy kept saying the light hurt his eyes.'

A cold chill of fear clutched at Rowan's heart. Please, God, she thought, please, God, don't let it be that—not that.

'Has he been sick at all, Mrs Dean?' she asked quickly. 'Complained of any back pain or a headache?'

'He was a little sick about an hour ago—nothing very much—hardly anything at all, really.'

'Any headache, pain in his back?'

'He did say his head and his back were sore earlier,' Fiona admitted, her face whitening still further.

Quickly Rowan pulled back the bed covers.

'You're not feeling very well, Billy, is that right?' she said softly as she ran her hands over his small, thin body.

The child didn't reply—indeed, he scarcely seemed aware of her.

'He's probably tired out after being so restless all night, Dr Sinclair,' Fiona Dean said, clearly torn between worry and hope. 'And they do say sleep's the best medicine when you're ill, don't they?'

'Where's your telephone, Mrs Dean?'

'It's in the sitting-room but the line went down after I phoned the surgery. Why. . .why do you need to use the phone?'

'I'm going to have to call out the air ambulance,' Rowan said as calmly as she could.

Fiona stared at her in panic. 'Oh, God, what's wrong? What's the matter with him?'

'I'll explain in a minute but I'll have to use my car radio first. No—you stay with Billy,' she added as Fiona made to follow her. 'It will calm him to see you there.'

Swiftly she ran out of the house. If her diagnosis was

correct, time was of the essence and she could only hope that they had enough of it.

Fiona Dean clutched at her arm frantically as soon as she returned to the bedroom.

'Tell me what it is—I want to know what it is!'

Rowan took a deep breath. 'I think. . .I think Billy may have meningococcal meningitis.'

'Oh, God, no!' Fiona wailed. 'Children die from that, don't they? I lost my husband in a car crash last year and I couldn't bear it if I lost Billy too—I just couldn't bear it!'

'Meningitis can be treated, Mrs Dean,' Rowan said soothingly, though in truth she was as panic-stricken as Billy's mother. 'Once he's in hospital—'

Fiona slumped into a seat. 'I should have phoned you earlier but I thought it was just flu. . . It looked like flu. Oh, God, Doctor, he mustn't die. . .he mustn't die. . .'

'He'll be all right—I'm sure he'll be all right,' Rowan broke in, gripping Fiona fiercely by the shoulders. 'But you mustn't panic—you mustn't show Billy how frightened you are—it doesn't help.'

Fiona wiped her face with a shaking hand, took a deep shuddering breath and nodded. 'How long. . .the air ambulance. . .how long will it take to get here?' she whispered.

'They'll be as quick as they can,' Rowan said reassuringly.

They had to be, she thought, they just had to be.

The minutes seemed endless. Fiona sat by the bed, her eyes fixed on her son's face, as though willing him to stay alive, and Rowan's attention was no less constant as she watched for any signs of deterioration.

And if he does get worse, her brain asked, what then? There's nothing I can do, nothing, she realised bleakly as she sponged the child's fevered forehead and listened and prayed for the comforting sound of a helicopter.

'I can hear a car,' Fiona Dean exclaimed suddenly.

'It'll be a neighbour. Could you talk to them, Doctor. . . explain. . .? I can't face anyone.'

Rowan nodded and went to the door, but it wasn't a neighbour—it was Ewan.

'Oh, Ewan, I've never been so pleased to see anyone in all my life!' she gasped. 'How did you know?'

'I heard your call on the car radio,' he said, his face grim. 'Are you sure about your diagnosis?'

She nodded.

'Rigid neck, inability to straighten his knees when you flex his hips—'

'Fever, headache, back pain. He has all the classic symptoms, Ewan.'

'Where is he?'

Quickly she led the way through to Billy's bedroom.

'Oh, Dr Ewan, it's bad, isn't it?' Fiona exclaimed as soon as she saw him.

'It's serious, yes, but, as I'm sure Dr Rowan has explained, meningitis is treatable and once the air ambulance arrives—'

'But how are they going to be able to land on such a day?' she protested. 'How are they even going to be able to see where we are? There's another three houses in the area—they could go to the wrong one.'

Rowan gazed at Ewan in desperation. She hadn't thought of that. If the helicopter landed at the wrong house they could lose vital minutes.

'Have you any white sheets, Fiona?' Ewan said quickly.

'White sheets?' she repeated in a daze.

'Sheets, blankets—anything big? If I lay them out on the field behind the house it will help the helicopter to see us.'

'The chest of drawers in the hall,' Fiona murmured. 'Look in there—there should be something.'

There was, but as Ewan carried a pile of sheets towards the back door Rowan stopped him.

'Let me do that—you stay with Billy.'

'But, Rowan—'

'Please,' she begged. 'You've more experience than I have. You stay with him—I'll make the signal.'

Indecision was plain on his face but eventually he nodded reluctantly and handed her the sheets.

She had known that it would be difficult on her own, but not just how difficult. Every time she thought that she had succeeded in anchoring one of the sheets under a stone a corner would wrench itself free and flail about wildly in the wind, beating at her legs and arms with incredible force.

Tears of frustration began to mingle with the raindrops on her face but she kept on going, knowing that she couldn't stop, knowing she couldn't give up—that somehow she had to succeed.

And then she heard it, the faint sound of the helicopter in the distance. She had done the best she could do; she could do no more, and quickly she stumbled towards the house.

Even now, the waiting was not over. Fiona Dean's cottage sat in a hollow at the foot of two densely forested hills. To reach the small field at the back of the house the pilot had to fly agonisingly close to the trees. Time and time again he hovered above them, only to pull back at the last moment.

Rowan watched with her heart in her mouth, knowing that if the pilot couldn't land she would have to drive Billy to Fort William, a journey that would take her over two hours—two hours that could mean the difference between life and death.

At last, after three nerve-racking attempts, the helicopter was down and Rowan sent up a silent prayer of thanks.

'I want to go with him—I have to go with him!' Fiona exclaimed as one of the medics ran from the helicopter and took Billy from Ewan's arms.

Rowan glanced up at the medic questioningly and he grinned.

'Room for a little one, I reckon,' he said.

Within seconds the helicopter was airborne again and within minutes it had disappeared into thick cloud, but Rowan didn't move. She continued staring up into the sky.

'You've done all you can,' Ewan said, touching her arm gently. 'You've given him the best possible chance by reacting so quickly.'

She nodded but all she could think of was how ill Billy had looked, how very tiny and vulnerable he had seemed in the arms of the huge medic, and how far away the hospital was.

'Will he be all right, Ewan?' she murmured.

'I don't know.' His voice sounded tired, bleak.

She pushed her soaking hair back from her forehead. 'Thanks for coming.'

'Hey, you're part of the team, remember,' he declared.

She tried to smile but as a rivulet of icy water ran down the back of her neck a violent sneeze overtook her and he shook his head in exasperation.

'You're soaked to the skin, aren't you?' he exclaimed. 'Look at you—dressed in that skimpy jacket and jeans, as though you were going for a stroll down Oxford Street. Don't you have any waterproof clothes?'

'No,' she mumbled, only to see him shake his head again. 'All right, all right. The first chance I get I'll buy some.'

'I'm going to make a country GP out of you if it kills me,' he grinned, 'but, in the meantime, I suggest you get back to your flat and into some dry clothes, or we'll have you down with flu next.'

She nodded, but it was easier said than done. No matter how many times she turned the key in the ignition, all she could hear was a dispiriting whine and then nothing.

'Don't keep on trying—you'll only flood the engine,'

Ewan advised as he watched her. 'I'll give you a lift back—my calls are finished for today anyway.'

They drove down the single track road in silence for a couple of miles, but the anger that had been building up in her since she'd diagnosed Billy's condition could not be contained.

'This whole situation—being so far from the nearest functioning hospital—it's just plain ludicrous!' she flared. 'Why can't Riochan be upgraded so we don't have to face situations like this? The people here pay taxes, for God's sake—they have a right to a better service!'

'I agree with you,' he said gently. 'I agree with everything you say but this is the reality of the situation here, lass, and we have to live with it as best we can.'

'But how many people have to be seriously ill—even die—before we get a better service?' she demanded furiously. 'Meningitis can kill or badly disable people if it's not treated quickly enough!'

'I know.'

His voice was constricted and she remembered all too late that his mother had died of meningitis.

'Oh, Ewan, I'm sorry!' she cried in consternation. 'Talk about insensitive...your mother...'

'It's all right, truly it is.'

'No, no, it's not,' she replied. 'I'm so sorry, so sorry, and for it to be Billy of all people—'

'Ironic, isn't it?' he interrupted with a short, bitter laugh. 'I've always said the main reason I've stayed here was to try and ensure that no other son had to go through what I did, and yet it's happened again—only this time to the son, not the mother.'

'Medical science has progressed so much in the last three decades, Ewan,' she said, desperately trying to sound positive. 'And the air ambulance will reach Fort William really quickly.'

'It's not the same as having a hospital close at hand, Rowan.'

It wasn't, and she knew it wasn't.

They drove back to Canna in total silence, both lost in their own thoughts, but when he drew his car to a halt outside the newsagent's she turned to him.

'Look, it's late and you must be hungry. Would you like to come up. . .share some dinner with me? It's nothing fancy... .just some stew left over from yesterday. And I could lend you a towel to dry your hair,' she added when he said nothing.

He smiled. 'Sounds like an offer I can't refuse.'

It didn't take long to slip out of her wet clothes and into a pair of warm trousers and a sweater but when she returned to the sitting-room it was to find that he had not only dried his hair but also put the casserole in the microwave and begun setting the table.

Her eyebrows rose. 'I'm impressed.'

'I'm not totally useless about the house,' he said, looking slightly aggrieved. 'And talking about being totally useless,' he added with a deep frown as he surveyed her, 'didn't it occur to you to dry your hair when you changed your clothes?'

'Yes, but—'

He didn't wait to hear the rest of what she'd been about to say, he just unceremoniously threw his towel over her head.

'I can do that!' she protested as he began drying it.

'Yes, but when?' he demanded. 'Next week, next month? You're an idiot—do you know that, Rowan Sinclair, a twenty-one carat idiot!'

'And you're so perfect, are you?' she chuckled. 'Hey, could you make that a little gentler, please—I'd like to be left with some hair!'

She heard him laugh, but as his touch became gentler, then rhythmic, then almost caressing, a shudder ran through her body. He was standing so close to her that she could see his chest rising and falling rapidly and could hear that his breathing was slightly uneven.

Her mind told her that she should tell him to stop—that her hair must be dry enough by now—but her body wasn't listening to her mind. Her body was urging him to continue—for his hands to slip down her neck, onto her shoulders, her waist—and then all at once he pulled off the towel, leaving her blinking in the light.

'All done,' he said with an effort. 'And that, if I'm not very much mistaken, is your microwave ringing.'

She went through to the kitchen, only to have to lean for support against one of the units. She wanted him—she wanted him so much—but she had to be able to trust him, and part of that trust depended on his telling her why he'd hit Colin.

They barely exchanged more than a few words as they ate their meal, but by the time they'd finished she had made up her mind.

'Ewan. . .about Colin. . .'

'I've nothing to say, Rowan,' he interrupted, his voice implacable.

'Well, I have,' she said determinedly. 'You're not a violent man—I'd bet money on you not being a violent man—and yet you deliberately set out to make the two of us the talk of the place. I wouldn't mind being the source of all this gossip if it had something to do with me—'

She came to a dead halt as he glanced away from her quickly but not quickly enough.

'Oh, God, that's it, isn't it?' she whispered, her cheeks scarlet. 'Colin said something about me, didn't he?'

'No,' he said swiftly—too swiftly.

She took an uneven breath. 'It must have been pretty bad. . .what he said. . .for you to hit him.'

He reached across and clasped her hand tightly in his. 'People say things they don't mean when they're hurt and angry.'

'Do they?' she muttered, staring steadfastly down at her plate, all too aware that she could probably guess what Colin might have said.

He lifted her chin. 'Oh, lass, if I were to believe only half the things that have been hurled at me in my time by some of my girlfriends, I wouldn't be able to hold up my head.'

She gazed into a pair of blue eyes that were tender and a face that was gentle, and a crooked smile appeared on her lips.

'You're a rotten liar, Ewan.'

'Selfish, thoughtless, uncaring—those are about the only accusations I'd care to repeat.'

'The rest are worse?'

'They are,' he smiled.

'But why?' she asked, puzzled.

For a moment she didn't think that he was going to answer and then he shrugged.

'I've told you before, Rowan, I can't and won't compromise.'

'I guess I'm a bit pigheaded myself,' she sighed and then chuckled as his eyebrows rose. 'OK, so I'm very pigheaded, but, Ewan...what Colin said...was it about...?'

'Forget about Colin,' he insisted. 'All that matters to me is now—not your past. And speaking of now,' he added ruefully, 'I'd better get going.'

And he would go, she realised. No matter how much he might want her he wouldn't pressurise her by making the first move—she would have to.

She took a deep breath. 'You don't have to go, Ewan.'

'Have you seen the time—?'

'I meant...I mean you don't have to go at all,' she said, her cheeks burning.

He searched her face. 'Are you saying what I think you're saying?' he said softly.

She nodded.

'And you're sure?'

'If you want God's honest truth, no, I'm not sure,' she said shakily. 'In fact, I'm terrified.'

'Of me?' he frowned.

Her face softened. 'No, not of you, never of you, but you see, Colin. . . Colin was the first. . .the only man. . . I've ever made love to and to get that close to someone again. . .it scares me a bit.'

'You're not the only one to be scared,' he grinned. 'I'm bloody terrified!'

She shook her head. 'You can't be—men aren't.'

'Why aren't they?'

'Because men are more. . .I mean they're designed to be able. . .I mean they don't. . .' She came to a tongue-tied, crimson-cheeked halt to see that he was laughing. 'Oh, you wretch—you know perfectly well what I mean!'

'Men can't be nervous about making love because they can perform with anyone?' he suggested.

'Well, can't they?' she said curiously.

'This man can't,' he smiled. 'Call me old-fashioned, if you want, but I'm afraid I have to care—really care about a woman—before I could make love to her.'

'But I thought—'

'You thought all men were superstuds?' he said, his blue eyes dancing.

'Something like that,' she blushed.

'We're as nervous as women when it comes to the crunch,' he replied. 'Even more so nowadays, when every damn woman's magazine is full of articles on THE IMPORTANCE OF A SUCCESSFUL SEX LIFE IN A RELATIONSHIP.'

'Oh, now I know you're not telling the truth,' she laughed. 'There is no way you'd ever go into the newsagent's in Canna and come out armed with women's magazines, Ewan Moncrieff!'

'Don't have to,' he said smugly. 'Ellie brings some in for the waiting-room and other kind-hearted souls do likewise. It's just a question of hanging about until everyone's gone home and then whipping the more interesting ones.'

'And did you learn anything from them?' she asked, her dimples dancing.

'Dammit, no,' he said ruefully. 'The only thing I ever learned was that if I didn't manage to give a woman multiple orgasms I must be a lousy lover.'

The laughter faded from her face.

She loved him so much—she wanted him so much—but how could she tell him that in the two years she'd been with Colin she'd never felt even the vaguest stirrings of an orgasm, far less experienced one, and, though Colin had been patient at first, eventually she'd found it easier simply to pretend than to face the inevitable inquisition?

She cleared her throat. 'Ewan, I'm not. . .I'm not very experienced. Colin used to say—'

'I don't want to hear what Colin used to say ever again,' he broke in firmly. 'Oh, lass, I know it's a big step, a big leap into the unknown,' he added as she gazed back at him, her cheeks flushed, her eyes nervous. 'After Jenny I thought no way am I ever going to put my heart on the line again. And then you came along, turning my life upside down, telling me I was dull and to lighten up. I'm prepared to take the risk if you are.'

'What if. . .?' Oh, God, this was so difficult to say, she thought. 'What if. . .if you find that I'm not. . .I can't. . ?'

He put his fingers against her lips.

'It doesn't matter if we don't set the heather alight this time, lass, let's just have some fun trying.'

'Fun?' she echoed.

'Making love should be fun, don't you think?'

She gazed at him uncertainly. She'd never found it so in the past, ever, but he was holding out his hand to her and she knew that there was no going back.

And it was fun. Never had she thought that making love could involve so much laughter, but with Ewan it did. When her single bed proved too narrow and they rolled out onto the floor she gazed up at him in wide-eyed consternation, only to see him dissolve into helpless laughter. When he discovered that tracing the slender contours of her thighs with his lips didn't turn her on, but instead reduced her to a fit of uncontrollable giggles, a deep throaty chuckle came from him.

It was as though they were both on a journey, a journey of mutual discovery, a journey in which love and laughter were irrevocably linked. She'd never been asked before what she did and didn't like and she'd never been bold enough before to ask a man the same questions, but gradually she came to realise, to her surprise, that to this man her needs and desires were more important than his own.

Time and time again he took her to the edge of the precipice, only to bring her breathlessly back down again, until deep within her a small flame began to stir, a flame that grew and grew in intensity. She didn't know what it was—she couldn't even have described what it was.

All she knew was that when he finally possessed her, her whole body suddenly exploded into a throbbing, con-vulsive ecstasy and she cried out for the first time in her life and clung to him, her face wet with tears, and acknowledged what she had known for such a long time—that she loved him, only him.

CHAPTER NINE

SUNLIGHT was streaming through her bedroom window when she woke the next morning and, for a split second, she wondered if it might all have been a dream—but it wasn't a dream. The presence of a warm body next to hers and a strong encircling arm round her waist told her that.

For a moment she lay motionless, listening to his gentle breathing, and then slowly she twisted round to face him.

'I love you, Ewan Moncrieff,' she whispered and heard him sigh as though he caught some faint echo of her words.

Gently she smoothed back his hair but the action must have disturbed him for he slowly opened his eyes and a warm smile creased his face.

'Do you remember that heather I was talking about last night, Rowan Sinclair?' he murmured. 'We didn't set it alight, did we? We damn well torched it!'

She chuckled and then sighed as his arm tightened round her possessively. 'We've got to get up.'

'Why?'

'Because it's eight o'clock and surgery starts in an hour and we haven't had any breakfast yet.'

'Can't say I'm all that hungry,' he observed. 'What about you?'

'No. . .not especially,' she replied as he rolled her onto her back and then propped himself up on one elbow to gaze down at her.

'A whole hour,' he said thoughtfully. 'How on earth are we going to pass the time?'

'I used to play "I-spy" a lot when I was a child,' she

answered solemnly. 'Or, if we had some cards, we could play whist.'

'Damn,' he murmured, reaching down to trace the curves of her breasts with his mouth. 'Something as exciting as whist on offer, and wouldn't you just know it—I don't have a pack of cards on me.'

'Looks like it will have to be "I-spy", then,' she said with difficulty as his lips abandoned her breasts and travelled slowly downwards.

'"I-spy" it is,' he agreed. 'The *adult* version, of course.'

'I didn't. . .I didn't know there was such a thing,' she said shakily, only to gasp out loud as his lips reached and then probed her soft mound.

'Oh, I can teach you a whole new set of games, lass,' he said, raising his head to smile at her—only to utter a muttered oath as the phone sprang to life. 'There are moments when I wish we'd gone into dentistry instead of medicine, Rowan Sinclair,' he sighed as he rolled onto his back, 'and this is surely one of them!'

Reluctantly she threw back the covers, grabbed her dressing-gown and went to answer it.

'What is it—what's wrong?' he asked, seeing her face when she came back.

'Oh, Ewan—I'm sorry, I'm so very sorry, but that was Tilly. Geordie. . .Geordie died in his sleep last night.'

His face twisted and she sat down on the bed beside him quickly. 'Look, I'll go for you—'

He shook his head. 'I have to do it—I owe them both that. My morning surgery—'

She put her arms around him. 'I'll take it for you.'

'I knew it was coming, I knew it was inevitable, but I hoped. . .' His voice faltered and he turned away from her quickly. 'I'm sorry. . .I never wanted you to see me like this. . .'

'Like what?' she protested. 'Showing me you loved him, showing me you cared? No, don't—please don't shut me out, Ewan,' she cried as he tried to shrug himself out of her arms. 'Let me help you, let me share your grief—don't, please don't shut me out!'

He gazed at her, his blue eyes showing such pain that it tore at her heart, and then he buried his face in her neck.

'It's all right,' she murmured over and over again as grief convulsed his powerful frame. 'It's all right, I'm here. . .hold on to me.'

And he did. He held on to her as though she were his only lifeline.

'Will it be Billy next?' he said at last, his voice thick with emotion. 'Will the hospital ring and tell us?'

'No,' she insisted as she dashed a hand over her wet cheeks. 'He's a strong little boy—a fighter. Think of all he's survived in his short life. He isn't going to die and he isn't going to be brain-damaged either,' she added firmly as he opened his mouth. 'He'll be all right—trust me.'

'Oh, lass, what would I do without you?' he said, holding her tight. 'What would I do if you weren't here?'

'Get blind drunk, I reckon,' she smiled tremulously.

He laughed huskily. 'You're probably right.'

'Look, are you sure about going out to the croft to sign the death certificate?' she continued as he reached for his clothes. 'I can do it for you. . .'

'It has to be me—Tilly would want it that way,' he replied. 'And thanks, lass,' he added, getting to his feet and kissing her hair lightly.

'What for?'

'Just for being you,' he said simply.

From her window she watched him leave, her heart going out to him. All the joy of the day had gone for him and she would have given anything to spare him this, but there was nothing she could do but be there for him if he needed her.

'What are you doing here this morning?' Ellie said

curiously as she swung into the office. 'I thought you were doing evening surgery?'

Quickly Rowan explained.

'Ewan will take this hard,' Ellie sighed. 'He was very fond of both Tilly and Geordie.'

'I know.'

'I heard about Billy Dean,' the receptionist continued. 'Has there been any word from Fort William about his condition?'

Rowan shook her head. 'I'll give the hospital a ring after surgery. Which reminds me—could you phone the garage for me and ask about my car? If it's going to be off the road for long I'll need to hire one.'

Ellie nodded. 'Something the matter?' she asked, seeing a slight frown appear on Rowan's forehead as she stared into the waiting-room.

'Has no one told Mrs Ross that only guide dogs are allowed in here?' she demanded.

'No one tells Mrs Ross anything,' Ellie said ruefully. 'Desdemona goes everywhere with her.'

'Not into my consulting-room she doesn't,' Rowan declared. 'And you can tell her I said so,' she added as Ellie stared at her uncertainly.

Morning surgery wasn't busy but Rowan wouldn't have cared if it had been packed to overflowing. Though she was sad about Geordie, she felt wrapped in a bubble of happiness that nothing could puncture.

Not even Freddie Thomson's long diatribe against the falling standards of the NHS depressed her, and when Mrs Ross came into her consulting-room, her Pekingese still in tow, she was only mildly irritated.

'This isn't the vet's, Mrs Ross,' she observed.

'Sorry?' the woman replied blankly.

'Skip it,' Rowan sighed. 'What can I do for you?'

'I thought Dr Ewan was taking surgery this morning— he's not ill, I hope?'

'He's fit as a fiddle, as far as I know,' Rowan replied,

all too conscious that Mrs Ross's eyes were fixed on her speculatively. 'Now, how can I help you?'

'He got his car fixed, then?'

'His car?' Rowan exclaimed, totally thrown.

'Well, I happened to notice that it was sitting outside the newsagent's all last night and I thought to myself, poor Dr Ewan, car broken down—that's really going to make life difficult for him.'

'I see,' Rowan murmured. 'Now, what seems to be the trouble, Mrs Ross?'

That Mrs Ross considered her a very poor source of information was evident, and that she was frustrated by her answers was equally clear.

'I've got this rash, Doctor,' she said almost angrily. 'It will be from those dreadful Moffat children, of course—running wild everywhere, spreading their germs. I wouldn't be at all surprised if they've given me the measles. Do you know the family at all?'

'Indeed I do,' Rowan replied as she examined the pink spots on Mrs Ross's arms. 'They're a nice family.'

'*Nice?*' Mrs Ross exclaimed, her small mouth twisting with distaste. 'They're totally out of control. Time and time again I've said to Alan Moffat that he should discipline them, but does he listen to me? No, he does not! Now I'm not one to gossip, Doctor, but that family—'

'Do you have the rash anywhere else?' Rowan asked quickly.

'It's on my legs as well,' she declared. 'It almost drove me mad last night, I can tell you—itch, itch, itch. And talking of last night,' she added, her brown eyes fixed once more on Rowan, 'wasn't it lucky Dr Ewan broke down right outside your door?'

'Was it?' Rowan replied, steadfastly staring at Mrs Ross's legs.

'Well, it gave the poor man somewhere to shelter, didn't it?' Mrs Ross continued. 'He did take shelter with you, didn't he?'

'You'll be pleased to hear you definitely haven't got the measles, Mrs Ross—'

'It must have been quite late before you managed to get to bed yourself, Doctor,' Mrs Ross observed thoughtfully. 'I remember looking at my watch when I was walking Desdemona and thinking, half past eleven and not a light on in Dr Ewan's cottage. Poor Dr Rowan must be wanting to get to bed and she can't until Dr Ewan leaves.'

'You've got fleas, Mrs Ross, dog fleas,' Rowan declared, 'and I'm rather afraid I think I'm looking at the source.'

Mrs Ross's eyes followed Rowan's down to a scratching Desdemona, and livid colour suffused her already florid face.

'Are you suggesting. . .are you implying. . .?'

'I'm sorry, Mrs Ross, I can give you some lotion to ease the irritation, but you'll need to drop in on the vet on your way home for some flea powder.'

Mrs Ross drew herself up to her full five feet, attempted to say something, failed, and swung out of the door with a still-scratching Desdemona in her arms.

A deep chuckle came from Rowan's lips, a chuckle that was still there when Ellie put her head round the door.

'What on earth did you say to Mrs Ross?' she demanded. 'She gave me such an earful when I asked if she needed another appointment!'

Rowan shook her head. She would have loved to share the joke but knew she couldn't.

'Any word about my car, Ellie?'

'It's outside. There wasn't much wrong with it, apparently—something to do with the points and the wet weather. Shall I get you a coffee or do you want to phone Fort William first?'

She didn't want to phone Fort William at all in case the news was bad but she knew that she had to.

'Coffee later, Ellie,' she said with an effort and then reluctantly reached for the phone.

Billy was in Intensive Care and was as well as could be expected. That was all they would tell her.

Slowly she got to her feet and went to stare out of her window. Make him get well, she whispered. Make him get well—for Ewan's sake as well as his own.

She was so deep in thought that she didn't hear her consulting-room door open, but she felt the strong hands sliding round her waist and the rough harshness of a tweed jacket against her back and turned quickly, concern plain on her face.

'How did it go, Ewan?'

'It was OK.'

'Truly?' she said, searching his face and seeing new lines there, lines of fatigue and pain.

'Tilly was wonderful—a hell of a lot better than I was,' he murmured, gathering her to him and resting his chin on her head. 'The funeral's on Thursday. Would. . . would you come with me?'

'Of course I will,' she said, tightening her hold on him. 'What about Billy—is there any news?'

'Just the standard hospital reply, I'm afraid—he's as well as can be expected.'

He sighed deeply and she wished that she could say something, do something, that would ease his pain.

'This couldn't have come at a worse time for us, could it?' he said into her hair. 'I should be concentrating on you, thanking you for the pleasure you gave me last night—'

'It's all right,' she said, pulling back from him slightly. 'Last night. . .last night was the most wonderful night of my life and nothing can ever take that away.'

'You're sure?'

'Do you have to ask?' she smiled.

'I won't be able to see much of you for the next few

days. . . Tilly will need me and there's the funeral to arrange. . .'

'Ewan, you don't have to explain. I know where your priorities lie right now,' she said softly.

He ran his finger along her lips gently, his eyes tender. 'Oh, lass, I love you—'

'I'm sorry,' Ellie said breathlessly as she came into the room at a run, 'Mary Rutherford from Laith—her husband's tractor's overturned and it looks serious.'

Immediately Rowan reached for her bag, only to feel Ewan's hand over hers.

'We'll talk later?' he said, his eyes capturing hers.

There was such love in his face that her heart turned over and she smiled and nodded.

But they didn't talk later—there never seemed to be the time.

Every spare minute Ewan had saw him either out at Tilly's croft or driving down to Fort William to sit with Billy Dean's mother. Rowan didn't mind—in fact, she loved him all the more for his consideration towards others—but with every passing day it became harder and harder for her to hug her secret happiness to herself.

She wanted to shout it from the rooftops; she wanted to run out into Canna's main street and tell everyone— 'I love him, I love him so much, and he loves me!'

'Something's happened, hasn't it?' Matt commented as he came into her room on the morning of Geordie's funeral. 'Between you and Ewan, I mean.'

'What makes you say that?' she said evenly.

'Oh, come on, Rowan,' he protested. 'You've got a smile on your face all the time and Ewan can't take his eyes off you for a minute!'

'Any fresh news about Billy?' she asked, deliberately changing the subject.

Matt gave her a very hard stare and then shook his head. 'Just the usual—he's as well as can be expected— but it's early days yet, Rowan.'

She nodded.

'It's good of you to go with Ewan to Geordie Wilson's funeral,' he continued.

'I can't say I'm looking forward to it,' she sighed. 'I've never been to the funeral of one of my patients before.'

And she hadn't. In London it had been much easier to divorce herself from her patients' lives. Living in one part of the city and working in another, she seldom saw her patients socially—had never really got to know them as individuals as she had done here.

'I've some news that might cheer you up,' Matt declared.

She raised her eyebrows questioningly and he grinned.

'The entire female population of the Western Highlands is shortly to be plunged into deepest mourning,' he exclaimed dramatically. 'There'll be a wailing and gnashing of teeth, of course, but even the best of us gets caught eventually.'

She stared at him in bewilderment and then her eyes lit up.

'Is this your convoluted way of telling me you've asked Ellie to marry you and she's said yes?'

He nodded.

'Oh, congratulations!' she cried, hugging him. 'I really do wish the two of you the very best of everything. You be good to her, do you hear me? She's a nice girl and I want to see her happy.'

'I love her, Rowan, and I'll make her happy, I promise.'

'I can't believe you're actually going to get married,' she exclaimed, shaking her head in wonder. 'Matt Cansdale, living in quiet domestic bliss—it doesn't sound possible.'

'Well, it is, I can assure you—though we'd rather you didn't tell anyone just yet,' he added. 'Ellie wants to tell her parents first.'

'My lips are sealed,' she smiled.

'We were rather hoping you and Ewan might have some good news to share with us,' he continued, his eyes fixed on her.

'Why's that?' she said lightly.

'Well, there've been whispers in the village that a certain Dr Ewan seems to visit a certain Dr Rowan rather a lot—especially in the middle of the night.'

Mrs Ross, she thought with irritation. It couldn't be anyone else but Mrs Ross.

'So?' he asked, his eyes dancing.

'So, mind your own business,' she replied and saw him laugh.

'OK, if you don't want to tell us, don't,' he declared. 'But what about a kiss for me, rather than just a hug by way of congratulation?'

She chuckled and kissed him warmly, only to hear a deep cough behind her.

'Ewan!' Matt beamed as he and Rowan turned to see him standing on the threshold, his expression decidedly dark, the line of his mouth grim. 'Come and congratulate me—Ellie and I are getting married.'

'Ellie and you?' Ewan repeated, and then strode towards him and grasped Matt's hand with a broad smile. 'How on earth have you managed to keep that one under wraps?'

'Oh, you can achieve just about anything with a little imagination,' Matt grinned. 'And I have to say I can heartily recommend falling in love. You should try it, Ewan,' he added slyly. 'I could give you my little black book—I shan't need it any more.'

'I sincerely hope not,' Rowan replied with mock severity and then caught sight of the time. 'We'd better get going, Ewan—the service starts at eleven, doesn't it?'

He nodded and led the way out to his car.

'Ellie and Matt,' he said thoughtfully. 'Who would have believed it? They're such complete opposites.'

Just like you and me, she thought, but she didn't say that.

'Do I look OK?' she said instead, gazing down at her dark blue suit. 'I don't want to cause offence but the only black things I have are sweaters and trousers and I didn't want to wear them.'

'Tilly won't care what you're wearing,' he replied. 'She'll just be pleased you came.'

'How's she coping?' she asked as they set off for the cemetery.

'A lot better than I am. She has a strong faith and that's holding her together.'

He looked so tired that she instinctively placed her hand gently on his arm.

'It was the best way, Ewan,' she said softly. 'For him to die peacefully in his sleep—it was the best and kindest way. We can't cure everybody and Geordie had a long and happy life—'

'I know that,' he interrupted harshly. 'Just as I know it's selfish of me to wish him back just because I miss him but, oh, how I miss him, Rowan.'

'I know you do,' she said as he drew the car to a halt outside the cemetery, where a large group of mourners had already gathered.

He turned to her, his blue eyes strained. 'Thanks for coming with me.'

She wanted to say, I'd go to the ends of the earth with you, Ewan Moncrieff, but she just smiled and tightened her grip on his arm.

The funeral service was a simple one, and all the more moving because of it. Ewan gave the eulogy, managing to evoke both tears and laughter as he described his long friendship with Geordie, and when a lone piper played 'Amazing Grace', not a few handkerchiefs were produced at the sight of Tilly Wilson, tiny and frail, but still indomitable at the foot of the grave.

'Thank you both for coming,' she said as Ewan and

Rowan stood by her as the other mourners began to take their leave. 'I know how busy you are and it's much appreciated, I can assure you.'

'It's our privilege to be here, Tilly,' Ewan said, his eyes kind.

She stretched up and touched his cheek with her frail hand.

'You're a good boy, a good boy,' she nodded. 'I was right about Geordie, wasn't I, Rowan? He stayed with me until the daffodils came.'

Rowan's grey eyes clouded. 'I'm so sorry, Tilly.'

'What for should you be sorry, my dear?' she exclaimed. 'Geordie's gone to his Maker where there's no more pain and sorrow. I'll join him soon—'

'Oh, Tilly—'

'Don't upset yourself, my dear,' she interrupted gently. 'There's no need—truly there isn't. Geordie and me, we shared many happy times together and I know we'll have many more in the next life.'

Rowan swallowed hard. 'Have you made any plans—decided what you're going to do now?' she asked.

'I'd like to move down to the village. I don't want to stay on in the croft—it wouldn't be the same without Geordie—but I don't want the house standing empty or, even worse, just to be used as a holiday cottage.'

A sudden thought came into Rowan's head. 'Do you know Alec Mackenzie at all, Tilly?'

'Aye, I do—a good man, if a bit short-tempered.'

'Would. . .would you consider letting him have the croft? He has farming experience and a young family who would just love to live in the country, I'm sure.'

Tilly gazed at her for a moment and then nodded. 'Tell him to phone me—'

'I'd rather Ewan did that,' Rowan said quickly. 'Alec and I. . .we're not on the best of terms.'

'So I heard,' Tilly replied. 'So wouldn't it be better if you told him, by way of making amends?'

Rowan shook her head. 'He might refuse to phone you if I suggested it—think I was offering charity.'

'If you say so, my dear,' Tilly sighed, 'though I have to say I think you're wrong. And now I'd better be going,' she said with an effort. 'Ewan, could you ask them to bring the car round to the gate for me?'

He nodded but as he went to do as she asked Tilly caught Rowan's hand in hers quickly. 'I sent him away, lass, because there's something I want to say to you, something I didn't want him to hear.'

'Is there something wrong?' Rowan asked with concern. 'Are you not feeling well—?'

'I'm fine,' Tilly said firmly. 'All I want to know is how you feel about him.'

A faint flush of colour swept across Rowan's cheeks and unconsciously her face softened.

'So it's like that, is it?' Tilly said with satisfaction. 'Oh, I'm no going to say anything to anyone if that's what you're feared of,' she added, seeing Rowan's embarrassment. 'I just wanted to know that when I'm gone there'll be someone watching out for him, and I was hoping it would be you. You love him?'

'Oh, yes, Tilly,' Rowan murmured. 'I love him so much it hurts at times.'

'Then hold on to him, lass,' Tilly said urgently. 'He might try and drive you away—oh, he wouldn't do it willingly,' she added, seeing Rowan's confusion, 'but he's a stubborn man, a stupid man, at times. Hold on to him, don't let him go.'

'I won't,' Rowan declared, 'but why would you think he'd try to drive—?'

'The car's at the gate,' Ewan said as he joined them. 'I'm sorry we can't come back to the house with you, Tilly.'

'Don't concern yourself about that,' Tilly replied. 'Just try and get some roses into this girl's cheeks before I see her next—she's too pale by far.'

They waited until Tilly's car had disappeared into the distance, before making their way to the small car park beside the cemetery.

'That was a grand idea of yours—suggesting to Tilly that she offer the croft to Alec,' Ewan said as he opened the car door for her, 'but I still think you should give him the good news.'

She shook her head. 'I'd much rather you did it.'

He shrugged. 'OK, if that's what you want, but I think it would be rather nice if people were to know it was your idea.'

An involuntary chuckle broke from her as he started the car. 'I think quite enough people are talking about me already.'

'Because I hit Colin, you mean?'

She shook her head again. 'That's old gossip, Ewan— the latest is considerably juicier, I can assure you!'

'What gossip are you talking about?' he frowned as he drove out onto the road leading back to Canna.

'The gossip that is wondering what you and I got up to all Monday night in my flat,' she said, trying to look severe and failing miserably. 'Your car is too recognisable, Ewan. You should have moved it.'

The car came to a screeching halt. 'Oh, damn and blast,' he groaned.

'It's OK,' she smiled. 'I don't mind, honestly.'

'But I do,' he protested, and then his lips curved into a grin. 'It looks like I might have to make an honest woman of you.'

Her heart turned over but she managed to laugh shakily. 'There's no need for that. Being known as Canna's scarlet woman sounds rather dashing to me.'

'Well, it doesn't to me,' he said firmly. 'The quicker I get a ring on your finger the better.'

'Are you. . .are you asking me to marry you?' she said uncertainly.

He put his hands on her shoulders.

'Rowan Sinclair, you're the best thing that's ever walked into my life, and I'm not going to lose you. We are going to have the church wedding, the cake, the ushers, the whole damn jamboree—and we'd better have it quickly because if we don't all of Canna will soon be talking about the fact that I can't keep my hands off you.'

'Just a minute,' she laughed, resting her hands against his chest. 'Are you asking me to marry you to save your face or mine?'

'Both,' he grinned. 'So will you do it—will you marry me?'

There was nothing in the world she wanted more but she couldn't resist teasing him just a little.

'Give me three good reasons why I should,' she asked, schooling her features into carefully balanced consideration.

'Well, I've given you one—the fact that if we weren't in this car, in full view of any passing public, I'd drag you down onto the floor and make mad, passionate love to you.'

'Pure sexual attraction,' she said dismissively, though her eyes danced. 'Give me another reason.'

'Because we're so right for one another,' he replied. 'Because in you I've finally found a woman happy to share my life here in Canna.'

'And anywhere else too,' she smiled.

'No, not anywhere else,' he declared. 'Here—right here. Think of the good we could do, Rowan—'

'You make it sound as though I'm marrying Canna, as well as you,' she chuckled.

'I guess you are in a way,' he said with a smile.

A tiny niggle of unease crept into her heart. 'But Canna's just a place—we might leave here some day.'

'We wouldn't.'

'We might.'

He shook his head. 'I'd never leave, you know that.'

Her hands slipped slowly from his chest. 'What if I wanted us to leave, Ewan?'

'You wouldn't.'

'But what if I did?' she insisted.

'Then I'd talk you out of it.'

'And if you couldn't?'

'Rowan, this is stupid,' he protested. 'Why are you getting so hot under the collar about some hypothetical situation that will never arise?'

She took a slightly uneven breath. 'Because you suddenly seem to be making an awful lot of assumptions on my behalf, Ewan.'

'What kind of assumptions?' he asked, his face stiffening slightly.

'That we'll work here because that's what you want; that we'll never leave here because that's what you want.'

'Do you want to work somewhere else?'

'Not at the moment, no,' she replied, feeling slightly foolish. Let it go, Rowan, she told herself, let it go, but she couldn't. 'All I'm saying is that I'd expect any decisions about our future to be joint ones, Ewan. I won't have my life dictated to by someone else. I had enough of that from Colin.'

'Oh, now you're being silly,' he exclaimed. 'It's not the same thing at all. Colin wanted you to give up your work—I'd never ask you to do that.'

Maybe she was just being silly but the words she'd said to Colin, that loving someone—really loving them—meant loving them without conditions, had come all too vividly into her mind.

'Do you love me, Ewan?'

'Oh, lass, do you have to ask?' he demanded.

'Then don't do this,' she murmured. 'Don't ask me to marry you and then place conditions on me.'

'But I'm not,' he protested.

'You are—can't you see that you are?' she cried. 'You're telling me that if I marry you I'll have to fit into your world, that I'll have no right to contribute to any decisions about our future, and if I don't agree to that then it's goodbye, Rowan.'

'You make it sound like I'm giving you an ultimatum.'

'Aren't you?'

'No, of course I'm not!' he exclaimed.

'Ewan, what if I said that unless we move down south to work I won't marry you?'

His eyes left hers and he stared out of the car window, his expression dark. 'Then we'd have to go our separate ways.'

Her stomach lurched uncomfortably. 'You mean that?'

'I thought you understood my commitment here—'

'Ewan, do you really mean that?' she interrupted, feeling as though her whole world had suddenly slipped out of focus. 'Do you really mean that if I wanted us to move south you wouldn't want to marry me any more?'

He gazed at her for a long moment and then nodded.

'Take me back to Canna,' she said, her throat so tight that she could hardly speak.

'Rowan—'

'We're blocking the road,' she said, indicating the tractor behind them.

They drove back to Canna in total silence but the tension between them was almost tangible, and when she reached for the doorhandle he put his hand over hers quickly to stay her.

'Rowan, you said yourself you would probably never want to leave here. When we're married—'

She deliberately pulled her hand out from under his.

'We're not getting married, Ewan.' Her face was white but determined.

'But, Rowan—'

'We're not getting married because I don't know whether you want a wife or just a professional partner for Canna.'

'That isn't fair,' he said, his colour high.

'And you think you're being fair?' she exclaimed.
'Find yourself another wife, Ewan. This woman won't
play second fiddle to a village!'

'Rowan, wait!'

But she didn't wait; she just got out of the car and
kept on walking until she reached the safety of her flat.

She switched on the radio, only to switch it off again
quickly as a female singer launched into a sad love song.
In desperation she turned on the television, to find a
group of experts deep in debate on the best way to survive
a broken relationship.

'And what would you know?' she said with irritation
as she turned the programme off.

'You're cutting off your nose to spite your face,' her
mind cried. I know, I know, her heart answered, but
surely a good marriage was an equal partnership, not
a dictatorship, and if she gave in on this what other
compromises would Ewan expect?

So that's it, then? her heart whispered. It's all over
between you and Ewan?

A choking sob came from her.

'Yes, that's it,' she whispered to the empty room. 'It's
all over.'

CHAPTER TEN

THERE was scarcely any need for Rowan to ask Mairi
Fisher whether the pills she had prescribed were having
any effect—the broad smile on the girl's face told its
own story.

'I just wish I'd come to you ages ago, Doctor,' she
exclaimed. 'All that wasted time—suffering in silence—
it was so stupid.'

'How's the physiotherapy going?'

'Mrs Thornton's great—she notices straight away if
I'm not doing the exercises properly and puts me right.'

'So everything's fine?'

'Couldn't be better,' Mairi beamed. 'I feel like a whole
new woman and my husband says I look like one too!'
She got to her feet. 'It's wonderful news too about Billy
Dean, isn't it—him being out of Intensive Care, I mean?'

Rowan nodded. 'It will probably be about a year before
he's fully fit, but he isn't going to be left with any perma-
nent disability like deafness or brain damage.'

'I don't know how Fiona would have managed without
Dr Ewan,' Mairi observed. 'All those times he took her
to Fort William and sat with her—he's a very special
man, isn't he, Doctor?'

'Yes, he is.'

'Are you OK, Dr Rowan?' Mairi asked, gazing at her
curiously. 'You're looking a bit peaky, if you don't mind
me saying so.'

'I'm fine,' Rowan replied. 'Just a bit tired today,
that's all.'

'Well you'd better be careful, Doctor,' Mairi chuckled,
'because if you can't keep yourself in tip-top health, what
hope is there for the rest of us?'

Rowan smiled in return but when Mairi had gone she stared unseeingly at the folders on her desk.

She couldn't go on like this—she knew she couldn't.

She had to leave—but to go where, to do what? Anywhere's better than here, her heart cried, if all you can have of him is what you have now—a polite and distant colleague. Then give in, her heart whispered. Tell him you'll always stay here; tell him you'll accept whatever decisions he makes. I can't do that, her mind protested, I can't.

Wearily she got to her feet. There was only one thing she could do and it might as well be done at the practice meeting this morning.

It wasn't a long meeting but it seemed interminable. Only Matt seemed to have any enthusiasm, any energy. Rowan sat mostly silent and Ewan answered every question in monosyllables.

'OK, is that it?' Ewan asked at last with clear relief. 'Is there anything else either of you want to discuss this morning, or can we bring this meeting to a close?'

It had to be now, she knew it had to be now, before she changed her mind.

'There's just one thing,' she said with a calmness that she was very far from feeling. 'I want you both to know that when Hugh Fowler comes back from Canada next month I'll be tendering my resignation.'

Matt gazed at her in amazement. 'You're joking, aren't you?'

She managed a shaky smile. 'Afraid not.'

'But why?' Matt demanded. 'Has something happened—?'

'I'm just not cut out to be a country GP, Matt,' she broke in quickly.

'Oh, but that's nonsense,' he exclaimed. 'Ewan—tell her that's nonsense.'

'It's Rowan's decision,' Ewan said, his face an expressionless mask.

'Is that all you're going to say?' Matt protested, turning on him. 'Aren't you going to try to talk her out of it—?'

Rowan got to her feet quickly. 'I'm flattered you don't want me to go, Matt, but I've made up my mind and I think. . .I know it's for the best.'

'But, Rowan—'

She took one look at Ewan's closed face and fled.

A heavy silence hung over the staff-room after she'd gone and then Matt let out a low sigh.

'For an intelligent man you're behaving like one bloody great fool, Ewan,' he observed.

'Thanks for sharing that thought with me, Matt,' Ewan replied wryly.

'You're just going to let her go—no argument, no attempt to dissuade her?'

Ewan shrugged his shoulders. 'She's a free agent— she can do what she likes.'

'But you're in love with her!'

Ewan drained the remnants of his coffee in one. 'I'll get over it.'

'I'll remind you of that when winter comes,' Matt retorted, 'when all you have to take to bed for comfort is your damn pride and stubbornness!'

'Are you finished?' Ewan's voice was bored, dis-interested.

'Oh, yes, I'm finished,' Matt exclaimed, 'and I think you are too—at least as a likeable human being!'

He swung out of the door angrily and did not see Ewan stretch out his long legs and shift his shoulders as though to ease the tension in them.

She had made her decision, he told himself, and he would get over it; he would forget her. In time he would forget the feel of her smooth slim body beneath his. In time he would forget her heart-shaped face, her laughing grey eyes, her infectious chuckle. In time, he told himself, you could forget just about anything if you tried hard enough.

*   *   *

It was agreed that no one outside the practice should know of Rowan's intention to resign before Hugh Fowler returned. As senior partner he had the right to be informed first, but Rowan also knew that as soon as word of her resignation hit the streets the tongues would start to wag with a vengeance.

'Are you really sure about this?' Ellie asked some days later with eyes that saw too much. 'You don't think perhaps you should wait, see how things turn out?'

Rowan shook her head. 'I know what I'm doing and, believe me, it's the only way.'

Ellie sighed. 'I was so hoping. . .what with it being my engagement party next week. . . You are still coming to it, aren't you?' she added as she went through to the office to answer the phone. 'It wouldn't be the same without you.'

'Wild horses wouldn't keep me away!' Rowan smiled.

And they wouldn't. Though she knew that her decision to leave Canna was the right one, she was going to miss the place and it wasn't just because of Ewan. Her Wednesday clinic had thrived since Annie Galbraith's intervention; there were patients whose treatments were only just beginning to show results; and then there was Matt and Ellie. In the short time she'd been here she'd come to regard them both as friends.

'Something the matter?' she said as she watched Ellie's vain attempts to interrupt a seemingly endless flow of high-pitched words from someone on the other end of the phone.

'It's Jim Coghill,' Ellie declared, holding the phone out to her. 'I can't make a word of sense out of what he's trying to say.'

Rowan frowned but as she took the phone and listened to Jim she realised with a sinking heart that she could make all too clear sense of what he was saying. Ishbel's baby was on its way.

'What's wrong?' Ewan asked as he came into the

office in time to see her putting down the phone with a muttered oath.

'Ishbel Coghill's gone into labour.'

'No problem,' he replied. 'Matt will do the morning rounds for you.'

'That isn't what's worrying me,' she said as she reached for her bag. 'I wish to God she'd been sensible and agreed to have the baby in hospital. I wish she'd allowed us do an amniocentesis, and I wish I knew whether she was full term or not.'

'That's an awful lot of wishes,' he smiled.

'And I've an awful lot be worried about,' she said with feeling. 'What if she's early, Ewan?'

'Judging by her size the last time I saw her, I would think that's unlikely,' he answered calmly.

'But what if it isn't? And at her age—'

'Look, I know she's your patient,' he interrupted, 'but would you like me to assist?'

'Would you?' she exclaimed, relief flooding through her. 'I've only ever done two births on my own and both of them were in a hospital. I'm terrified and I don't mind admitting it. This baby means so much to both of them.'

'Right, then, I'll assist,' he declared. 'You go on ahead and I'll phone Riochan to tell them to have an ambulance ready on standby in case we need it.'

She turned to go out and then paused.

'Something else?' he asked, his hand on the phone.

'Just. . .just thanks,' she said.

'Any time,' he smiled. 'Now, you'd better get a move on or the newest member of the Coghill family may arrive before you do.'

I wish it would arrive before I get there, she thought ruefully as she drove at breakneck speed to the Coghills' house. At least then the responsibility wouldn't be mine any more.

In every dream she'd had of this moment everything

that could go wrong had gone wrong, and only last week she had still been attempting to persuade Ishbel to have the baby in hospital. Ishbel, however, had remained adamant. She wanted her child born at home and she wanted Rowan in attendance.

Jim Coghill flew out of the front door as soon as her car appeared in the drive.

'I've been timing the contractions, Doctor, and I think everything's as it should be, but I've never been so glad to see anyone in all my life!' he cried. 'She's in the bedroom—'

'I need to scrub up first, Jim,' she replied. 'Can you show me where?'

With clear reluctance he took her through to the bathroom.

'Couldn't you hurry up a bit please, Doctor?' he said impatiently as she washed her hands and arms thoroughly. 'I don't want to leave Ishbel too long on her own but she insisted I come out and meet you—she said I was driving her mad.'

Rowan chuckled.

'And I can't get her to lie down, Doctor,' he continued. 'All she keeps saying is that it's easier if she walks up and down, and I'm sure that can't be right—'

'Ishbel knows what's she's doing, Jim. If we keep her flat on her back it's like asking her to try to push the baby uphill. Squatting or half leaning against someone uses the force of gravity and it can make the labour shorter.'

He attempted a smile that deceived neither of them and then led the way through to the bedroom.

Ishbel's face was white but her eyes lit up when she saw her.

'So junior's decided to make his appearance when I should be doing the morning rounds, has he?' Rowan said with a smile. 'Not very considerate of him, I must say.'

'Or of her,' Ishbel gasped.

'Or of her, indeed,' Rowan nodded. 'Now, I just want to take a little look to see whether your cervix is dilated yet, Ishbel, so if you could hop on the bed for a moment for me. Good,' she added when she'd straightened up. 'Everything seems fine.'

'What does that mean—about the cervix being dilated, Doctor?' Jim asked anxiously as Ishbel began pacing the floor again.

'When the baby's ready to make its appearance Ishbel's cervix will widen to about ten centimetres so that the baby's head can pass through,' Rowan explained.

'Surely it must be wide enough by now?' Jim said, wiping his forehead with a handkerchief. 'This seems to have been going on for an awfully long time.'

Rowan shook her head and smiled.

'We've a long way to go yet, Jim, but Ishbel's going to be in safe hands. Dr Ewan's coming to assist me. He's just as keen as I am to see the newest member of the Coghill family make its entry into the world.'

Ishbel started to laugh and then her laugh was cut short as her face twisted with a contraction and she caught hold of her husband's shoulders in panic.

'Squat and breathe, Ishbel—remember what they taught you at the antenatal clinic,' Rowan said quickly. Breathe. . .breathe. . . Good, good, that's right. Now relax.'

'I don't need Dr Ewan,' Ishbel said raggedly. 'I know you'll see me right—you'll not let anything bad happen to me or the baby.'

Rowan bit her lip as she bathed Ishbel's damp forehead. All she could do was pray that Ishbel's confidence in her was not misplaced. Please, she thought desperately, please let nothing go wrong.

The next few hours seemed interminable. Ewan arrived but seemed content to play only a supportive role. Occasionally Rowan would look to him for confirmation of what she was doing but eventually she found herself forgetting that he was even there as Ishbel's contractions came closer and closer together and she knew that it would not be long.

'I can see the baby's head!' Jim Coghill cried at last with delight, peering over his wife's shoulder as she leant against him. 'I can see it, I can see it!'

'Just one more push, Ishbel,' Rowan declared. 'Just one more push—that's all it needs.'

'I can't, Doctor, I can't!' Ishbel sobbed, her hair plastered damply against her forehead.

'Yes, you can—you're doing beautifully,' Rowan replied encouragingly. 'Come on now—take a deep breath and then push as hard as you can—you can do it, I know you can.'

Ishbel took several shallow ragged breaths and then pushed down with all her might. She let out a cry that was halfway between a scream and a cry of exultation— and suddenly the baby was there.

Quickly Rowan cut the umbilical cord and then lifted the child in her arms and cleaned the blood and mucus from its face. For a moment there was no sign of life and then, as she continued to massage the child, a tiny wail of protest filled the bedroom.

'Is it all right, is the baby all right?' Ishbel cried as she lay back against her husband, totally exhausted.

Rowan looked down at the baby and then across at Ewan and felt as though her heart would burst.

'You've a beautiful baby girl, Ishbel,' she said huskily as she handed the tiny scrap of humanity to her. 'She's small but she's perfect, just perfect.'

'Oh, Doctor, thank you,' Ishbel whispered, gripping her hand tightly. 'Oh, Jim, look at her,' she continued, gazing up at her husband tremulously. 'Isn't she beautiful—isn't she the most beautiful baby you've ever seen?'

'I'll finish off in here for you, Rowan,' Ewan said quietly. 'Go and have a seat—you look exhausted.'

'I'm not tired—'

'Not now you're not, but I guarantee that once the euphoria wears off you'll feel like you've been hit by a sledgehammer!' he grinned. 'Oh, and Rowan,' he added as she turned to go, 'well done, lass.'

She beamed up at him, tears welling in her eyes.

She knew now with certainty that her place was in general practice. She wouldn't have exchanged the highest post anyone could have offered her for this one moment when her expertise counted—when her presence was needed and wanted.

This was what she had come into medicine for. She was Rowan Sinclair, general practitioner, and she was happier with that than she would ever have thought possible.

'Oh, Doctor, thank you!' Jim Coghill said, his voice filled with emotion as he came through to the sitting-room after her and shook her hand vigorously.

'It was your wife who did all the hard work,' she laughed. 'I'm just pleased everything turned out as it should.'

'We'd like to name our daughter after you,' he continued. 'Ishbel and I both agreed that if the baby was a girl she should be called Rowan as a token of our appreciation for all you've done for us.'

'But I've done no more than my job,' she protested.

'You were there whenever my Ishbel needed you, Dr Rowan, and we count you as a friend.'

Rowan gazed at him, quite overwhelmed.

'Will you both take a dram?' Jim added as Ewan joined them. 'Just to wet the baby's head?'

They nodded and as the glasses were raised to the new arrival Rowan didn't think she could have felt happier or prouder if it had been her own child who was being toasted.

'I wonder,' Jim said sheepishly, his eyes turning to the bedroom door, 'I wonder if you'd mind if I just slipped away for a moment? You see, the thing is I can't actually believe I've really got a daughter. . .'

'Away you go, you daft beggar,' Ewan grinned. 'We don't need entertaining, you know that.'

Jim nodded with obvious relief and disappeared back into the bedroom.

'Pleased, Rowan?' Ewan said as he sat down.

'Relieved would be a more accurate word,' she answered.

'You didn't need me here, you know,' he observed.

'Perhaps not, but it was good to know someone experienced was with me in case something went wrong,' she said.

'Actually, I've got a small confession to make regarding my experience,' he said wryly. 'You know you said you'd only ever done two births on your own? Well, I'm afraid I've only done two as well—one was forced on me when the ambulance arrived too late and the other was when I was training to be a doctor.'

'*What?*' she gasped.

'We're not exactly in frontier country here, Rowan. The vast majority of our patients prefer the technology of a hospital when they're giving birth.'

'Why you. . .you *fraud*!' she exclaimed, beginning to laugh. 'You gave me the impression—'

'I never said I was an expert on home births,' he laughed. 'You just assumed I was.'

'Talk about the blind leading the blind,' she declared. 'What would you have done if something had gone wrong?'

'Panicked first and then hoped that between the two of us we could sort it out.'

'Well, I'm just glad you didn't tell me that before or you wouldn't have seen me for dust!' she chuckled.

He grinned. 'In future I would suggest you ignore nine-tenths of what I say.'

'I fully intend to,' she smiled.

He gazed at her intently.

'Does that mean. . .does that mean you might reconsider and stay on in Canna?'

The smile on her face became fixed.

'We could do such good work here together, Rowan,' he continued. 'Here, patients are not just faceless numbers or a series of case notes but people, real people that you get to know and who become friends.'

'Ewan—'

'Oh, it's not easy—no one would pretend that,' he went on swiftly. 'Knowing your patients so well doesn't always bring joy—it can bring heartache too. But occasionally there are moments like this, when you've helped bring a new life come into the world or when you've discovered a tumour and know it can be treated, and then it's the best job in the world.'

She gazed at him silently. His face was so alive with enthusiasm, an enthusiasm she knew she shared, but it wasn't enough, it just wasn't enough. He was talking about his work—he was talking about Canna—not about her.

'I can't stay, Ewan.'

His face tightened. 'You're going back to London.'

'Does it matter where I go?' she asked wretchedly.

'I want. . .I want you to be happy, lass,' he murmured.

You're the only one who can make me truly happy, her aching heart cried, only you, no one but you, but you won't compromise and I can't.

She got through the next week on automatic pilot. She told herself that the overwhelming fatigue she felt was due to her work and to the fact that she was helping Ellie with her arrangements for her engagement party, but it wasn't the truth and she knew that it wasn't the truth.

It was the sleepless nights, the nights when she tossed and turned—imagining a life without Ewan—that were sapping her strength. That, and the heart-wrenching knowledge that Ewan appeared to be totally indifferent to her decision.

'There's still time for you to change your mind, you know—take back your resignation,' Ellie said on the evening of the party. 'No one knows—'

'I won't change my mind, Ellie.'

'But what are you going to do—where are you going to go?'

'I thought I might set up in general practice somewhere in the Scottish Borders or maybe Argyllshire,' Rowan replied and then laughed shakily as tears welled in Ellie's dark brown eyes. 'Hey, come on, tonight's your big night, remember? Don't worry about me—I'll be fine.'

And I will be fine, she told herself determinedly as she went home. I survived Colin. I can survive Ewan— I can survive anything if I have to.

The engagement party was to be a strictly informal affair and she'd decided on a fine woollen skirt with a high-necked silk blouse for the occasion, but the reflection that gazed back at her from her dressing-table mirror was not an encouraging one.

Not even her keenest admirer would have said that she was looking her best, she decided with a deep sigh. She'd never had much colour but these last few weeks had drained every vestige from her face, leaving her ashen.

Ruthlessly she applied some blusher to her cheeks, only to head for the bathroom immediately afterwards to wash it off again. She might look like a wan, dark-eyed ghost without it but at least that was better than looking like a clown.

The village hall was packed by the time she arrived. Everyone from the area had been invited and with the local band supplying the music for the Scottish country dances, the tables groaning with food, and the whisky flowing it looked as though it would be a night to remember.

Ellie's parents greeted her like old friends and there

were patients to talk to and laugh with so not for one moment was she allowed to feel like an outsider, but the one man her eyes followed all evening was the one man who seemed determined to avoid her.

She told herself that she didn't care that Ewan was dancing every dance with apparent relish, she told herself that she didn't care that he seemed to be perfectly happy without her, but even to her own ears the words had a hollow ring.

'I don't know what's he's trying to prove,' Ellie said in an irritated undertone as the evening wore on. 'He's not left the dance floor since he arrived and normally you'd have to twist his arm to get him to dance just once.'

'He's enjoying himself,' Rowan murmured, taking a deep gulp of her wine.

'Well, he's got no right to—no right at all,' Ellie protested. 'Oh, hell, no!' she added with exasperation. 'That's all we need tonight!'

Rowan turned quickly to see that Alec Mackenzie was striding across the floor towards them, looking grim but determined, and her heart sank.

'Now, look, Alec, I don't want any trouble tonight,' Ellie declared firmly as he stood in front of them. 'This is my party and I won't have it spoiled by anyone.'

'I only want to talk to Dr Sinclair for a minute,' he replied.

'Then come down to the surgery tomorrow,' Ellie exclaimed.

'What I have to say won't take long—'

'It's OK, Ellie,' Rowan said gently as the girl bridled visibly. 'Look, your mum wants you—I'll be fine.'

That Ellie was not happy was clear but eventually she went with a backward glance of concern and Rowan turned to Alec.

'What can I do for you, Mr Mackenzie?' she said with a calmness she was very far from feeling.

'I understand I've you to thank for the offer of Tilly Wilson's croft,' he said stiffly.

'Who told you that?' she demanded.

'Dr Ewan.'

She bit her lip. 'He was wrong to tell you and I'm sorry if you think I've interfered—'

'We've not seen eye to eye in the past, Doctor,' he interrupted, 'and I don't think we ever will over...over that matter with Frank Shaw, but I've just come to say I'm obliged to you and to shake your hand—if you're willing.'

She stared at his outstretched hand. For a proud man like Alec Mackenzie he was offering a lot.

'I'll shake hands with you any day, Mr Mackenzie,' she said, holding out her hand.

He took it, shook it firmly and then strode away, leaving her staring after him.

It was a special moment and she would have liked to have shared it with Ewan but he wasn't sharing anything with her any more, he was too busy throwing himself into yet another energetic eightsome reel.

She stayed a little longer in her quiet corner but eventually she could bear watching him no longer and went to find Matt and Ellie. They accepted her announcement that she had a headache without comment but she knew that their eyes followed her with concern as she slipped quietly away.

What did you expect? her heart asked as she let herself into her flat. You told him you wouldn't marry him, that you were leaving Canna, so what did you expect? For him to have cared just a little, she thought as she went through to the kitchen and plugged in the kettle. I hoped he might have cared, just a little.

She had just made herself a cup of coffee when the phone rang, and for a moment she considered ignoring it. It couldn't be a patient—Dr Swan from the neighbouring practice was providing emergency cover to enable them all to go to the party.

Talking to anyone is better than sitting here with nothing but your own thoughts to entertain you, her mind said, and she reached for the phone with a sigh.

'Rowan, it's Ewan,' a tense voice said at the other end of the line. 'It's Ishbel Coghill's baby.'

'What's wrong with her?' she demanded, her brain suddenly alert.

'I gather there's some problem. I'm going out there myself and I wondered—what with the interest you take in the family—if you'd like to come.'

'Pick me up,' she answered, slamming down the receiver.

As they drove along in silence her mind ticked off the possible medical conditions that could have affected Ishbel's little girl and none of them was encouraging. Surely nothing could have gone wrong—it would be too cruel after the Coghills had waited for so long to have a child of their own.

She was so worried that for a full half-hour she took no notice of where Ewan was taking her, but when her watch showed that they'd been travelling for over forty minutes a slight frown appeared on her forehead.

'Ewan, where are we going?' she demanded, peering out into the dark and trying, without success, to identify some landmark.

'We're almost there,' he replied and promptly pulled into a passing place.

'What's wrong—why are we stopping?' she said in confusion as he switched off the engine.

'I want to talk to you.'

She gazed at him open-mouthed for a moment and then her brows snapped down. 'We don't have time to talk. Ishbel's daughter—'

'Is probably fast asleep in her cot beside her doting parents.'

'Then why did you tell me she wasn't?' she protested. 'Why call me out if there's nothing wrong?'

'Because I had to talk to you and I doubted whether you'd want to talk to me after the way I treated you this evening.'

She took a deep breath. 'Take me back to Canna.'

He stretched out his long legs.

'Take me back to Canna, Ewan,' she repeated, her voice clipped. 'Now!'

Still he said nothing, and her temper broke.

'Right—give me those car keys,' she demanded, stretching over towards them, only to see him pull them from the ignition, roll down the window and toss them out into the darkness.

'Have you gone mad?' she exclaimed. 'It's pitch black out there—how the hell are we going to find them?'

'We'll find them in the morning,' he said, maddeningly calm.

She struggled to control herself and failed. 'If you think for one moment that I'm going to sit out here all night with you, then you need your head examined!'

'I don't see what else you can do,' he replied, examining his nails thoughtfully.

'Then watch me!' she retorted, opening the car door and getting out.

'I wouldn't recommend that, Rowan,' he declared. 'It's a long walk back to Canna and we have wild cats in the Highlands. I can't say I'd care to meet one on a dark night like tonight.'

She stared out into the gloom indecisively and then got back into the car and slammed the door shut.

'I'm never going to forgive you for this, Ewan Moncrieff,' she said tightly. 'Of all the stupid, infantile things to do—'

'At least you can't say it was dull,' he smiled, but she refused to be placated.

'Look at me, Rowan.'

When she didn't move he grasped her gently the shoulders and turned her to face him.

'Look at me,' he repeated.

Reluctantly she looked up into his deep blue eyes.

'I have tried and tried to convince myself that if you leave I can go back to living my life the way I did before but I can't, I *can't*,' he said softly. 'If you want to live and work in London, lass, then we will live and work in London. If you want to live and work in Timbuktu then we'll go to Timbuktu.

'Just tell me you love me and I'll go anywhere you want, as long as we can be together.'

'Do you really mean that?' she said uncertainly.

'More than I've ever meant anything in my life,' he declared firmly. 'Marry me, Rowan—no strings, no conditions—just marry me.'

'An equal partnership, all decisions made jointly?' she demanded.

He nodded. 'So, will you marry me?'

'Are there really wild cats out there?' she said suspiciously.

His lips curved. 'I doubt it very much.'

An involuntary chuckle broke from her. 'You're impossible, Ewan Moncrieff!'

'I know,' he said, shamefaced. 'Rowan—Rowan, do you love me?'

His blue eyes were fixed on her, hopeful, uncertain.

'Yes, yes I love you,' she said with a soft smile.

'And you'll marry me?'

'Oh Ewan, you're bad-tempered, arrogant, domineering, single-minded—how could I possibly say anything but yes?' she chuckled.

He drew her to him and his lips came down on hers in a kiss that left her reeling.

'Oh, Ewan, why did you have to throw the car keys away?' she sighed into his neck. 'We're going to be stuck out here until morning.'

He shook his head ruefully. 'Maybe that gesture was a bit stupid.'

She pulled back from him slightly. 'There's no "maybe" about it,' she declared. 'We're stuck here in the middle of nowhere, with nothing to do. . .'

She came to a halt as his lips curved into a very definite smile.

'Oh, no,' she said, her cheeks reddening. 'We can *not* do that. . .Ewan. . .Ewan, stop it!'

'Why?' he asked as he slowly and methodically began to unbutton her blouse.

'Because someone might come along,' she protested, ineffectually attempting to fend him off.

'So?'

'Ewan, if we're going to stay in Canna for ever more, we have our reputations to think of. . . Oh, Ewan, we *can't*. . .not in the car. . . Ewan, have you taken leave of your senses?'

'Completely and utterly,' he murmured as he drew her back into his arms.

And as he began kissing her again she decided that if this was insanity it was a lovely way to go.

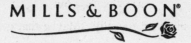

MILLS & BOON®

NOVEMBER 1996 HARDBACK TITLES

ROMANCE

His Cinderella Bride *Heather Allison*	H4548	0 263 15025 9
Substitute Bride *Angela Devine*	H4549	0 263 15026 7
Living with Marc *Jane Donnelly*	H4550	0 263 15027 5
Honeymoon for Three *Sandra Field*	H4551	0 263 15028 3
Bringing up Babies *Emma Goldrick*	H4552	0 263 15029 1
The Dominant Male *Sarah Holland*	H4553	0 263 15030 5
Too Wise to Wed? *Penny Jordan*	H4554	0 263 15031 3
Ryan's Rules *Alison Kelly*	H4555	0 263 15032 1
Misleading Engagement *Marjorie Lewty*	H4556	0 263 15033 X
Falling for Him *Debbie Macomber*	H4557	0 263 15034 8
The Second Mrs Adams *Sandra Marton*	H4558	0 263 15035 6
A Royal Romance *Valerie Parv*	H4559	0 263 15036 4
Gold Ring of Betrayal *Michelle Reid*	H4560	0 263 15037 2
The Unexpected Father *Kathryn Ross*	H4561	0 263 15038 0
The Baby Battle *Shannon Waverly*	H4562	0 263 15039 9
Second-Best Wife *Rebecca Winters*	H4563	0 263 15040 2

HISTORICAL ROMANCE™

Major's Muslin *Marie-Louise Hall*	M395	0 263 15089 5
Stolen Heiress *Joanna Makepeace*	M396	0 263 15090 9

MEDICAL ROMANCE™

Partners in Love *Maggie Kingsley*	D313	0 263 15075 5
Drastic Measures *Laura MacDonald*	D314	0 263 15076 3

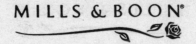

MILLS & BOON®

NOVEMBER 1996 LARGE PRINT TITLES

ROMANCE

HISTORICAL ROMANCE™

MEDICAL ROMANCE™

TEMPTATION®

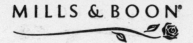

MILLS & BOON®

DECEMBER 1996 HARDBACK TITLES

ROMANCE

Valentine, Texas *Kate Denton*	H4564	0 263 15049 6
The Bride, the Baby and the Best Man		
Liz Fielding	H4565	0 263 15050 X
Living Next Door to Alex *Catherine George*	H4566	0 263 15051 8
A Wife of Convenience *Kim Lawrence*	H4567	0 263 15052 6
Maddie's Love-Child *Miranda Lee*	H4568	0 263 15053 4
Ending in Marriage *Debbie Macomber*	H4569	0 263 15054 2
Wicked Caprice *Anne Mather*	H4570	0 263 15055 0
A Lesson in Seduction *Susan Napier*	H4571	0 263 15056 9
Smoke without Fire *Joanna Neil*	H4572	0 263 15057 7
The Playboy *Catherine O'Connor*	H4573	0 263 15058 5
To Lasso a Lady *Renee Roszel*	H4574	0 263 15059 3
Marriage-Shy *Karen van der Zee*	H4575	0 263 15060 7
Hers for a Night *Kate Walker*	H4576	0 263 15061 5
Sophie's Secret *Anne Weale*	H4577	0 263 15062 3
A Convenient Bride *Angela Wells*	H4578	0 263 15063 1
A Husband's Revenge *Lee Wilkinson*	H4579	0 263 15064 X

HISTORICAL ROMANCE™

The Knight, the Knave and the Lady		
Juliet Landon	M397	0 263 15095 X
A Highly Irregular Footman		
Sarah Westleigh	M398	0 263 15096 8

MEDICAL ROMANCE™

A Surgeon to Trust *Janet Ferguson*	D315	0 263 15093 3
Wings of Passion *Meredith Webber*	D316	0 263 15094 1

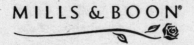

MILLS & BOON®

DECEMBER 1996 LARGE PRINT TITLES

ROMANCE

Grounds for Marriage *Daphne Clair*	959	0 263 14818 1
Running Wild *Alison Fraser*	960	0 263 14820 3
The Trophy Husband *Lynne Graham*	961	0 263 14855 6
Rendezvous with Revenge *Miranda Lee*	962	0 263 14822 X
A Proper Wife *Sandra Marton*	963	0 263 14910 2
Intimate Relations *Elizabeth Oldfield*	964	0 263 14823 8
Marriage by Arrangement *Sally Wentworth*	965	0 263 14824 6
Amber's Wedding *Sara Wood*	966	0 263 14825 4

HISTORICAL ROMANCE™

Ravensdene's Bride *Julia Byrne*	0 263 14898 X
King's Pawn *Joanna Makepeace*	0 263 14899 8

MEDICAL ROMANCE™

A Private Affair *Sheila Danton*	0 263 14832 7
Doctors in Doubt *Drusilla Douglas*	0 263 14833 5
False Pretences *Laura MacDonald*	0 263 14834 3
Loud and Clear *Josie Metcalfe*	0 263 14835 1

TEMPTATION®

A True Blue Knight *Roseanne Williams*	0 263 15023 2
Madeline's Cowboy *Kristine Rolofson*	0 263 15024 0